THE CROSSROADS

RAVEN'S WINGS SAGA: BOOK 1

EMILY DAVIDSON

CHAPTER 1

K illian Pendergast stood barefoot on his back porch, watching the sun come up over the lake. The pines stretched their long shadows toward him, swaying gently in the light breeze. He took a deep breath in, savoring the mingled aromas of the forest around him and the mug of coffee in his hand. When he'd had his fill of the view he went back inside to get ready for work.

He pulled on his park ranger's uniform: dark green pants, khaki button-up shirt, and sturdy brown hiking boots that were scuffed from so much use. They would be getting some more use today because it was his turn for foot patrol. That meant wandering the paths from one end of the park to the other, helping patrons as needed, and checking to make sure all the trail markers were still intact and no trees or other debris had fallen to block the way. To Killian, it didn't even feel like working.

He grabbed his keys from the top of the dresser and turned to leave, but the sound of movement from behind him made him turn back. Sarah was awake, but barely, looking over at him with a sleepy smile on her face.

"Hey there, Stranger Ranger," she said.

"Morning," he said, laughing at the memories that nickname conjured in his mind. "I didn't mean to wake you."

"That's alright. I should be getting up soon anyway. You're on foot patrol today, right?"

"Yeah."

"Be safe, okay?"

"Always."

He walked back over to the bed, kissed her goodbye, then left the house and drove the short distance to the park, where he checked in with the head ranger, Gavin, at the main lodge before setting out. The most exciting event of the first four hours was helping a cyclist repair a flat tire. Then, shortly after eleven o'clock, he got a call from Gavin over the radio.

"Where are you right now, Killian?"

"Almost to the lookout point. Why?" He didn't care for the tightly controlled urgency in Gavin's voice.

"We have a possible missing camper. He was staying near where you are right now. I've already briefed Rick on the situation and sent him up to the lookout, but could you meet him there? Two pairs of eyes are better than one."

"Of course," Killian said, speeding up his walk until it was just short of a jog. "What makes you think the guy is missing?"

"His car is still in the parking lot and his permit expired last night."

"Maybe he just lost track of time," Killian said, trying to ignore the bad feeling gnawing away at him.

"Maybe so, but I want you and Rick to check it out anyway. Let me know what you find."

"Yes, sir."

Killian and Rick arrived at the lookout at almost the same time, Killian on foot and Rick on one of the park's ATVs.

"Hey! Did Gavin call you?" Rick yelled over the growl of the engine.

"Yeah. You know where we're going?"

Rick nodded and gestured for Killian to hop on. It didn't take them long to reach the campsite, and what they found there wasn't good. There were wide tears in the side of the tent, which was unzipped and empty except for a sleeping bag. The rips in the canvas were grouped in fives, just like a bear's claws. Dented cans and torn food packages littered the ground at their feet. Rick squatted down, squinting at the jumbled tracks and trying to make sense out of them. After some time, he straightened back up.

"There are human tracks mixed in with the bear's, but I can't tell if they were made at the same time," he said. "We need to call this in."

"If it was a bear attack he probably didn't get far," Killian said, much as he disliked putting that thought into words.

"Like I said, there's a chance he wasn't here at the same time as the animal. Maybe he took a well-timed stroll," Rick replied, then placed a call to Gavin and explained the situation.

"Start searching the area around the campsite," Gavin

told them. "Work your way back toward the main part of the trail. If he's injured he probably headed toward people."

"Okay, boss," Rick replied. "We'll keep you updated."

"You boys be careful," Gavin said after a brief pause. "Our bear may still be around."

"You got it," Rick answered. Then he and Killian were left alone with nothing to hear but quiet birdsong and the wind rustling the canvas of the shredded tent.

"Where should we start?" Killian asked.

"There," Rick said almost at once, pointing to the far side of the clearing from where they stood. Seeing Killian's blank expression, he added, "What, you're telling me you can't see that trail?"

Killian looked closer, even closed one eye, but still he was forced to admit that he didn't see anything.

"You have much to learn, young padawan," said Rick, shaking his head in exaggerated fashion.

"Shut up, Rick," Killian replied, but there was no heat in his tone. He knew humor was Rick's way of dealing with stress.

"Over here, where the grass is all bent," Rick said, taking a few steps in the direction he was indicating. Now that he pointed it out, Killian wondered how he had missed it in the first place.

"No point in trying to take the ATV," Rick continued. "Looks like we're going on foot."

They set off into the closely growing trees, Rick leading and Killian following close behind with his head on a constant swivel. He was on the alert for anything that might help them in their search. But there was only the trail in front of them, and that petered out at the edge of a ravine about half a mile into the trees.

"So much for our trail," Rick sighed.

"Any idea which way he went?"

Rick took a few steps closer to the sharp drop-off, then took two hasty steps back and started fumbling for the radio at his belt. Killian moved forward and saw their missing camper lying in the slow-moving stream at the bottom of the little gorge. The water surrounding the man was bright red and Killian felt his stomach do a slow-motion flip. He turned his head and willed himself not to lose his breakfast. He wasn't sure how long he stood like that before Rick punched him in the arm to get his attention.

"There's a way down over there." Then he took a closer look at Killian's face and added in a much different tone, "Hey, are you okay?"

"Fine," Killian snapped, almost defiantly. He gave a hard swallow, tasting coppery fear. "Let's go."

They began to pick their way down to the bottom, moving as quickly as they could while still being cautious. As they got closer they could make out a pair of binoculars around the injured man's neck.

"Looks like it might not be a bear attack at all," Killian said. The only wound he could see was a gash in the man's scalp. "Maybe he was birding and lost his footing."

"Who cares how it happened?" Rick replied, sparing the sky a passing glance. "He still needs help."

Killian glanced up as well, looked back down at his footing, then stopped and craned his neck upward once again. About half a dozen birds were circling directly over the spot where the unfortunate camper lay. At first he

assumed they were vultures, but they were too small—
they looked more like ravens. And why hadn't he seen
them from a distance?

"Killian, come on!"

He hurried to catch up to Rick and they approached
the injured man together. As they got closer, they were
both encouraged by the rise and fall of the man's chest. It
was shallow and uneven, but it was definitely there. Rick
got on the radio to Gavin again and Killian dropped to his
knees beside the man in the stream. In addition to the
head wound, there was a deep cut along the side of his
chest; it looked as though he'd been caught by a sharp
rock while sliding down the side of the ravine.

"Sir? Can you hear me? We're here to help you, just
hold on a little longer."

The man's eyes opened and his pupils ranged slowly
from side to side. It was impossible to tell if the movement was random or if he knew someone was there with
him. Then the lids slipped closed again.

"Get him talking," said Rick, slinging his backpack off
and getting out the first-aid kit.

"Can you tell us your name, sir?" asked Killian.

The man gave a weak cough, spraying blood. Then he
said, "Ryan. I'm… Ryan Delving."

It was clear that each word cost him great effort.

"My name's Killian. My friend Rick and I are going to
help you."

"They're already here. The odedaud." Killian wasn't
sure he'd caught that last word correctly. "Good. That's
good."

"What's he saying?" asked Rick, but Killian only shook

his head. Ryan coughed again, and then said something so low Killian had to lean in.

"What was that, Mr. Delving?"

"Find… John. Tell him… I'm sorry."

He breathing grew ragged and he said no more.

"Check his pulse for me," said Rick, moving around to Ryan's head to examine the gash there.

For a moment, Killian was afraid to do as Rick asked; he felt an overwhelming urge not to touch the injured man in front of him. Then he brushed aside his fear, reached out, and took hold of Ryan's wrist. He felt a weak pulse, but only for a moment—it faltered, and the next second it was gone entirely.

"Rick, his heart just stopped!" Killian was barely able to get the words out through the shock. Had they come so far just to watch someone die right in front of them?

"Move," said Rick, and his calm tone helped Killian quell the panic that was threatening to overwhelm him. He got out of the way and Rick started CPR, issuing orders as he worked. "Get back to the campsite. Gavin and an EMS crew will meet you there. Tell them what happened, and then lead them back here."

Without a word, Killian began scrambling back up the rocky path to the top of the ravine. In a way he was glad of the treacherous footing, because it gave him something to focus on besides the doubts swirling through his mind. Had he done something wrong? Was it *his* fault the man down there was dying?

Don't be stupid! he told himself. *All you did was check his pulse.*

It didn't take long for Killian to reach the campsite and then lead Gavin and the paramedics back to the ravine, but it was clear that they were too late. Rick's hands were on his knees and his head was bowed. He spoke without looking up, but they could tell he was crying.

"I did everything I could. But it wasn't enough."

Killian wiped moisture from his own eyes and looked up at the mockingly perfect sky. There were no clouds to be seen up there.

No birds either.

The rest of that day passed in a haze of law enforcement officials and paperwork. First, there were forms for the park, to inform management about what had happened. Then, there were statements and reports to be filed with local law enforcement. Next, the coroner came and asked them all manner of questions, most of which Rick answered since he was the main one who had attempted first-aid. They had thought the coroner would be the last interested party, but then the state police showed up and it was back to square one, going over every detail of what had happened.

He slipped and fell. What else is there to say? Killian found himself thinking at one point.

It seemed there was a great deal more to say, both in writing and by means of a formal interview. Rick and Killian were called in separately for the latter.

Probably want to make sure our stories match up, Killian thought as he and his interviewer sat down in Gavin's office. *You'd think we were criminals instead of two guys who just tried to help.*

"Has anything like this ever happened during your

time here?" asked the woman who was taking his statement.

"No," Killian replied.

The officer continued to study him with a sympathetic look in her eyes. Killian shifted in his seat and dropped his gaze.

At last she said, "I know how hard it can be. We can wrap this up tomorrow if you'd prefer."

"No," Killian answered firmly. "Let's just get it over with."

And the litany of questions began. When at last it was finished, Gavin called Killian and Rick into his office.

"I won't keep you long," he said, gruff as always. "I just wanted to thank you both for everything you did today. You handled an incredibly difficult situation very well."

"Thanks, boss," Killian said hoarsely. Rick was uncharacteristically silent.

"You should also know that I don't want to see either of you back at work until Monday. Is that understood?" When they had both nodded, Gavin went on, "Go home. It's been a long day for everyone."

Outside in the parking lot, Killian frowned at his friend's pale, dazed face and shell-shocked eyes.

"Are you okay to drive, Rick?"

Rick's mumbled answer was addressed to the keys he was bouncing up and down in his cupped palm.

"Don't have much of a choice. Lisa's working late tonight, so short of calling a cab…"

Get in," Killian said, opening the passenger door of his truck.

"Thanks," Rick replied.

It was the only word spoken for the first half of the journey. Then abruptly, Rick said, "You know I actually considered going into medical school at one point when I was younger?"

"Really? What made you change your mind?"

"The thought of losing a patient," Rick answered. "I didn't think I would handle it very well, having to explain to someone's family that their loved one was dead because of something I did, or didn't do."

"Rick," Killian said, and then stopped when he realized he had no idea what to say to comfort the man sitting beside him.

"Don't say, 'It wasn't your fault,' " Rick replied harshly and they lapsed into silence once more. When he finally spoke again, he asked, "Do you think he had a family?"

"I didn't notice a wedding ring," Killian said. "But he mentioned someone named John."

"He did?"

"Yeah. Just before he... before I checked his pulse. He said to find John and tell him sorry."

"Did you tell the cops?"

"Yeah. I'm sure they'll find him, whoever he is."

"What else was it that he said to you? Something about someone already being there?"

"It sounded like 'odedaud,' " Killian replied, frowning. "But I don't have a clue what he meant. Besides, there was nobody around except us and the birds."

"What birds?" Rick asked, and Killian took his eyes off the road briefly to stare at him.

"You're telling me you didn't see that flock circling above the ravine?"

"No. I didn't see anything."

They fell silent once more, with Killian strangely troubled by what Rick had said. If it had been just one bird he would have understood, but a whole group like that? Rick had looked up at the sky only a moment before him, so he should have seen *something*. For some reason, thinking about it made Killian's skin want to break out in goosebumps.

Rick thanked him again for the ride when the pulled into his driveway a short while later.

"You gonna be okay until Lisa gets back?" Killian asked.

A ghost of a smile crossed Rick's face and Killian was glad to see it. "I'm a big boy. I think I can handle myself. Guess I'll see you next week."

"Yeah. Good night, Rick."

CHAPTER 2

I t was only when Killian pulled into his own driveway about half an hour later that he realized he had never called Sarah to tell her what had happened, or that he was going to be late getting home. He walked through the front door and let the screen bang shut behind him, still trying to figure out how to break the news to her.

"Hey, Killian, is that you?"

"Yeah, it's me. Sorry I'm late."

"Did Rick have car trouble or something?"

"Huh?"

Sarah came around the corner from the kitchen, wiping her hands on a dishtowel. "I called up to the lodge a little while ago, just to see if you had left yet. Gavin said he saw Rick get into your car, so I thought—" She broke off as she took a closer look at him, her eyes widening at the sight of his heavily soiled uniform. He was covered in mud and sweat, and there was blood on his shirt. She stepped forward slowly and traced the stain with her fingertips.

"The blood isn't mine," he muttered, gently removing her hand. "Or Rick's, if that's what you're thinking. I—I'll just go and change real quick. If I have time before dinner, that is."

"Yeah, of course. I'm just finishing it up."

When Killian entered the kitchen a few minutes later, now wearing jeans and an old T-shirt, there were two steaming plates of food and two cold bottles of beer set out on the table. They sat down together, and Sarah stayed quiet, giving him time to gather his thoughts.

"This looks good," Killian said, taking an unenthusiastic bite of casserole to put off the moment when he would have to relive the day one more time.

"It's okay if you don't want to talk about it," said Sarah.

That simple remark was what finally sent Killian's wall tumbling down. He felt Sarah's arms slip around his shoulders and he hugged her back, hard, while hot tears leaked out from beneath his closed eyelids. Eventually they broke apart.

"Sorry," Killian croaked, using his napkin to clean himself up.

"You don't have to apologize for being human, babe." Sarah paused, and then asked, "Do you want to tell me what happened?"

"Gavin didn't say anything when you called?"

"No. But he sounded tired. Not like his usual self."

"That's understandable," said Killian, and he told her everything about what had happened. The only thing he left out was the mysterious birds that were apparently only visible to him. He couldn't explain to himself why he was leaving them out—it was just a deep instinct that he

13

felt he needed to obey. When the tale was told, Sarah laid her hand over top of his.

"I can't even imagine. That must have been awful."

"Not as awful as it was for Ryan Delving. Not as awful as it will be for any family he has."

When he saw the hurt, confused look on Sarah's face, Killian sighed.

"I'm sorry," he told her. "I've just always had a problem with people putting the focus on me during a bad situation."

"I never knew that."

"Yeah," Killian replied, rolling his fork around in his fingers and not looking at his wife. "I sort of had a meltdown at my dad's funeral. I was only about six at the time, so nobody blamed me, but I still felt bad that Mom had to stop and look after me when she was already so sad herself."

"Maybe you were helping her without even realizing it." Seeing his blank look, Sarah continued, "Maybe caring for someone else was a distraction. So she wouldn't have to think about being sad for a little while."

"Maybe you're right," Killian said, wondering how that idea had never occurred to him in the almost twenty years since his father's death.

"My mom was sort of the opposite of yours," Sarah said. Now she was the one toying with the food on her plate instead of eating it.

"What do you mean?" Killian prompted her when she didn't speak again right away. It cost him a lot of effort to focus on her, but she had helped him so he was determined to return the favor. She looked up at him and smiled.

"Do you remember the night we first met?"

"You were looking for owls up on the ridge," Killian said, with a reminiscent smile. "I offered to walk you back to your car because it was getting late."

"My hero, the Stranger Ranger," she said, and they both laughed a little.

"That was one of the best nights of my life," said Killian.

"It was one of the worst of mine up until you came along. Mom and I had just had a huge fight, because I didn't tell her I was driving across two states to go try and spot some birds. I just packed up and left. The owls were only part of the reason for the trip anyways—most of it was just to get away from her. Dad was the one who sort of held us all together. After he was gone... Well, you know how it is between me and her."

Killian nodded. He had always known about the tension between his wife and his mother-in-law, but had never realized how deep it ran.

"The night I met you, she told me my father would have been ashamed of the way I'd been acting since he died. She didn't know..."

"Didn't know what?" Killian asked.

Sarah's voice broke as she answered, "That... that Dad always said he would take me out to that ridge one day so we could watch the birds together, just the two of us. But he never got the chance."

Killian could not think of an adequate response, and she was unable to say anything else. But he reached out and squeezed her hand, and a wordless understanding passed between them.

"Looks like tears are better medicine than laughter in this household," Sarah said after a little while.

"Wonder what that says about us?" Killian asked in reply, and then they finally did laugh. The spell didn't last very long, but it gave Killian hope that maybe he would be able to sleep that night after all.

When Killian woke up the next morning his head was spinning with half-remembered dreams, most of them about birds. And yet he still didn't want to ask Sarah about the birds he'd seen yesterday, although she probably would have been able to tell him all about them—she taught an ornithology course at the local community college every semester, along with some other classes. Sarah was just finishing her breakfast when he wandered into the kitchen.

"Morning," she said, looking up from her bowl of corn-flakes. Killian returned the greeting and went to the coffee pot. "Did you sleep okay?"

"Better than I thought I'd be able to," Killian answered. "I guess talking last night did me some good."

"It helped me, too," Sarah replied, and that was all that was said on that subject. Then she asked, "So, what are you going to do with your day off?"

"I don't know," Killian answered. "I might go into town and visit the library. Find a good book to distract me."

"That sounds nice."

"You want to meet up for lunch later?"

"I can't. I have office hours today."

"Ah, okay."

"And speaking of the office," she said, consulting her watch, "I'd better go so I can get everything settled for my first class. I'll see you later tonight."

CHAPTER 3

Killian spent the morning going through some of Sarah's ornithology books, thinking he might get lucky and find a species that looked like a large raven but behaved like a bird of prey. When that didn't pan out, he drove into town, got a bite to eat, and then strolled into the public library. Sitting down at one of the computer terminals, he pulled up the library's searchable database and keyed in the mysterious word—odedaud—that he thought Ryan had said.

Although he tried it with several different spellings, the only result that came up was a suggestion that perhaps he had made a typo and was really looking for something else. He finally gave up and started searching for general ornithology books instead. He doubted these would help him, but he still scribbled down several likely call numbers and set off to collect his findings. He had just picked up the first one when he heard a familiar gruff voice coming from the next aisle.

"We should get you caught up on some recent events," Gavin said.

"But why?" a younger-sounding voice replied. "I got a pretty good perspective as an odedaud."

Killian dropped the book he was holding, causing a passing library aide to give him a reproachful glare. He picked up the volume, tried to force his face into an apologetic expression, and then hurried around the corner. Gavin was turned away from him.

"—might be listening!" Gavin was saying. The young man he was speaking to had sandy hair and green eyes and looked to be about Killian's own age, maybe a little younger. He was dressed in old jeans, a faded polo shirt, and a jacket that Killian recognized as Gavin's. It hung off his small and skinny frame.

"Hi, Gavin," said Killian, taking a step forward. Gavin spun around.

"Oh… Killian. What are you doing here?"

"Decided to do some reading on my day off."

"Reading about birds? I'd have thought you could do that at home."

"None of the books Sarah has mention a species called the odedaud."

Both Gavin and the younger man flinched.

"How do you know that word?" Gavin asked. His voice was pitched so low that Killian had to move closer to make out what he was saying.

"The man that died yesterday. He looked up at the sky and said something about how the odedaud were there." Killian shrugged and continued, "It may have just been his head wound making him talk nonsense, but what can I say? I got curious."

"How did you—" Gavin's companion began, but Gavin laid a hand on his forearm to silence him.

"This isn't the place to talk about it." He paused, frowning at the ground, and then looked up again. "Will you come to the park at eight o'clock tonight?"

Killian was tempted to demand answers now, but a closer look at Gavin's face told him that his boss would do this his way or not at all. With no other choice, he agreed to the time and place of the meeting.

"Good. Then I'll see you tonight," Gavin said. "Oh, and Killian? Don't mention any of this to Sarah, or anyone else. Especially not that word."

"Why not?"

"Because you could be putting both them and yourself in danger. Good bye, Killian."

Gavin beckoned to his companion and they walked away. Killian watched them go, and then looked down at the book in his hand. After a brief internal debate he dropped it on the nearest book return cart to be reshelved. He would be getting answers tonight, and if he didn't the book would still be here tomorrow. He strolled over to the mystery section and pulled out a book without even looking at the title—it would be a mystery even to him. He found a chair, settled down, and opened it. He'd only meant to sit there long enough to read a few pages, but he ended up reading five chapters in that one sitting. He checked the book out and headed home.

Sarah got back from the school about an hour and a half after he did, bearing a large, grease-spotted bag of Chinese food.

"Hope this is okay for dinner," she said, holding it up

for his inspection. "I just don't feel up to cooking tonight."

"Like I'd ever turn down Chinese takeout," Killian replied. "Everything go alright at work?"

"Yeah. I'm just a little behind. I meant to grade midterms during my office hours, but I had to deal with a panicking freshman girl instead."

"What was she so panicked about?"

"She had a 'B' in the class instead of an 'A.' So naturally she thought it was the end of the world."

"Sounds like me," said Killian, taking the various cartons out of the bag and setting them on the table. Killian relished the normalcy of the routine, the normalcy of the conversation. It felt wholesome somehow, especially when he compared it to the previous day.

"Yeah, sounds like me, too." They both laughed, and it was a good and genuine sound. They sat down to eat and Sarah went on, "So because of that I now get to spend my entire evening reading papers about various bird species of the Pacific Northwest."

For a split second Killian was almost overcome with the desire to ask her about the birds he'd seen; after all, she had just given him the perfect opening, and it wasn't like he would have to mention the name. The moment passed when he remembered the grave look on Gavin's face that afternoon. He would just have to live with his curiosity for a few more hours.

"While you're doing that," he said, "I've got to go and see Gavin."

"Really? Why?" She looked up, surprised.

"He didn't say exactly," Killian answered, choosing his words with care. "Just that it had something to do with

21

what happened yesterday. He asked me to swing by the park after it closed tonight."

"I hope it's nothing too serious," Sarah said, frowning in concern.

"I'm sure if it was he would have just told me."

"Yeah. I guess you're right."

Silence fell between them for a little while and Killian was left to wonder why Gavin *hadn't* just told him. Why had he and the young guy he was with looked so frightened of that mysterious word? And who was Gavin's companion anyway? Killian was almost certain he had never seen the boy before, but he still looked familiar somehow. With an effort, Killian pushed these questions aside and talked about mundane, everyday things with Sarah until it was time for him to leave.

At a quarter to eight, he got in his truck and drove to the park. The main lot was empty except for Gavin's car. There was a "Closed" sign on the door of the lodge, but Killian saw lights on inside. Gavin was behind the counter of the gift shop, counting up the day's sales and donations. Killian tapped on the glass and Gavin waved him in.

"Prompt as ever, I see."

"Like I said, I got curious."

Gavin grunted in response. "You may wish you had left well enough alone by the time we're done talking."

"That just makes me even more curious." But Killian's grin faded when Gavin did not smile. "What's going on, Gavin? What's so dangerous about all of this?"

"Let's wait for John to get back, shall we?"

Gavin led the way over to a cluster of chairs that were arranged around a coffee table in the middle of the room.

A puzzle piece clicked into place in Killian's mind as they sat down.

"The man from yesterday. Ryan Delving. He said, 'Find John.' Is that who you were with at the library?"

"Yes," said a quiet voice from behind Killian.

Killian stood up and watched John walk over. They shook hands and John joined their circle. Both younger men instinctively looked to Gavin to begin the meeting, but when he showed no signs of speaking, it was Killian who broke the silence.

"So how did you know Ryan?"

"We're family," John answered. "Or at least we were."

"I'm sorry for your loss. Was he your grandfather?"

"My dad," John answered. Correctly interpreting Killian's frown he added, "Technically speaking I'm almost forty."

"You look like you're in your early twenties."

"I'm twenty-four actually, but I'll take the compliment."

"I thought you just said you were forty."

"Well, my mind is forty but this body is only twenty-four." He broke off with a frustrated sigh. "Oh, I don't know. It's hard to explain when I don't completely understand it myself. I honestly don't even know where to start."

He looked at Gavin again, and this time Gavin actually spoke. "You were right about the creatures Ryan mentioned being birds," he began, but John interrupted.

"It's okay to use the word now." Gavin raised his eyebrows, and John continued, "Edmund said he'd guard us."

"Who's Edmund?" Killian asked blankly.

23

"He's an odedaud. One of the birds."

There was a pause. Then Killian said, "And he's talking to you right now?"

"Yes," John answered calmly. He rubbed at his temples briefly and then added, "Right now you're worried about my mental state, and you're trying to figure out how to best express that to Gavin without me noticing. Am I right?"

"How did you know that?" Killian asked.

"Edmund just looked inside your mind and told me what he found."

"So you're hearing the voice of a telepathic bird?"

"Yes."

"Maybe you're just good at reading people."

"Or maybe I'm telling the truth. For example, how else would I know that your wife sometimes calls you the 'Stranger Ranger'?"

Killian's mouth dropped open. He looked uncertainly at Gavin, who shook his head.

"Don't look at me. I didn't tell him."

Killian looked back at John and said, "Edmund again?"

"Actually I picked that one up for myself, yesterday. Until then I was an odedaud, too."

It took Killian a while to find his voice again. When he had, he said, "So... you were there at the park yesterday? You saw the whole thing?"

John nodded but did not speak.

"That's awful," Killian said. He felt sick to his stomach at the thought of what John must have gone through, having to witness that.

"All part of Sven's plan, I'm sure."

"Sven?"

But John suddenly clutched his head with both hands as though suffering from a migraine. Gavin and Killian watched him in concern.

"Alright, alright, I'm sorry," said John, seemingly to himself. Then he dropped his hands back into his lap, looked up, and said in a normal tone of voice, "Best not to mention that name again. Too much risk of being overheard."

Gavin nodded as though that comment made complete sense to him. Killian was still confused but decided not to press the issue. He had bigger questions on his mind.

"How did you become an odedaud in the first place?"

"Fifteen years ago my father had a near-death experience. I struck a deal: my soul for his."

"So you were a bird for fifteen years, and your human body didn't age or decay during that whole time?" Killian asked skeptically. "You were just immediately able to get up and start walking around? I thought people who were in comas for a long time had muscle deterioration and stuff."

"Apparently those rules don't apply when you're an odedaud. My dad had an old hunting cabin near here. That's where I woke up." Slowly, John reached inside his jacket and pulled out a thick wad of envelopes, all of them unopened. He riffled through them and said, "He came to visit me once every year, to check on me and leave me a letter, telling me what I'd missed. These are all I have left of him now."

In the silence that followed John's statement, Killian's cell phone rang, making all of them jump. Looking down at the screen, Killian saw it was Sarah.

"Excuse me a second," he said, getting up and walking

25

a few steps away. Then he answered the call and put the phone to his ear.

"Killian?" Sarah asked before he could say anything. Her voice was high and panicky.

"What is it?" he asked urgently. In his peripheral vision he saw Gavin watching him closely and John rubbing at his temples again. "What's wrong, Sarah? Are you okay?"

"I don't know," she answered and he could tell she was holding back tears. "I don't think—"

The line didn't go dead, but there was a muffled thump and then silence. Killian called her name a few times, but there was no response. He hung up and turned around to see that both John and Gavin were on their feet.

"I need to get home right now."

"I think it was my fault," said John, with a stricken look on his face. Then his eyes glazed over and he added, "You were right."

"Right about what?"

"Not you. Edmund. He's talking to me telepathically."

"Never mind that now, let's get moving," said Gavin. "I'll drive."

He hastened out to the parking lot, John and Killian scrambling to catch up.

"Did your wife know why you were coming here tonight?" asked John as they piled into Gavin's car.

"No. I just told her it was something to do with what happened yesterday."

"And she didn't know the name odedaud?"

"No." Killian paused and then asked, "What did you mean when you said it was your fault?"

"Sven must have heard me mention his name."

"Then why is he going after Sarah?"

"Because he knows you know too much, so he's using it as an excuse to teach you a lesson. But as long as we follow the rules, he can't hurt her."

"What kind of rules?" Killian asked, desperately trying to keep up.

"She has to survive on her own for an hour. We can't make any move to help her or her life is forfeit."

"Wait a minute," Killian said slowly. "With your dad, yesterday—I took his pulse. Did I kill him by doing that?"

"Don't you dare put that on yourself," Gavin answered before John could speak. "Sven is the one who killed Ryan, not you."

"Actually... that's why Sven is so upset with you," said John. "He wanted my father's death to be drawn out, for him to suffer, and then you came along and helped to end his pain. I'm the real reason he killed my dad."

Gavin said, "Did you not listen to a word I just said, boy? It wasn't Killian's fault, and it wasn't yours." Without giving John a chance to respond, he continued, "Right, so here's the plan. We get to Killian's house, assess the situation, and call for help as soon as the one-hour time limit expires." He consulted his watch. "That should be in about forty-eight minutes from now."

John's hands stole up to his temples again and he said, "Fifty-two minutes actually."

"Are you sure?" Killian asked.

"Yes."

"Fifty-two minutes, then," Killian said, looking at his own watch.

Gavin said, "We can talk some more while we wait. If you want to."

When they reached the house Killian was out of the car and running to the front door almost before Gavin could get the engine turned off. He stopped dead when he got to the living room and saw Sarah on the rug, unconscious, her phone inches from her right hand. That explained the thump he'd heard. He turned around when he heard Gavin and John enter the room behind him.

"Your old boss did this to her?" Killian asked.

"Yes," John said.

"I thought it was against the rules to deliberately cause harm to someone," said Gavin. His tone was so calm they might have been discussing the correct way to play a board game, rather than the cosmic limitations of a group of creatures that shouldn't even exist.

John gaped at him and then said, "That rule can be broken if there's a risk for exposure. But how do you know so much about this stuff anyway? I thought my dad told you what he knew, although God knows where he got his information from. But there's no way he could have known that."

Killian walked away from the other two to kneel at his wife's head. He wanted to brush her long, dark red hair out of her face, make her more comfortable, but he didn't dare touch her. There was silence for a while and then he looked up at Gavin, who had not answered John's question.

"You said we'd talk while we waited. Start talking."

Gavin sat down on the couch and gave a long sigh. Then he said, "You have things backwards, John. Your father got his information from me, not the other way around. And I know about all of this because I used to be an odedaud myself. I became human again about twenty years ago."

John had been standing until the point, but now he collapsed onto the arm of Killian's favorite chair, staring at Gavin with his mouth hanging open.

"So that's how you knew what would happen to me after my father died."

"Yes."

"Anyone want to explain to the non-odedaud in the room how Ryan's death had anything to do with John turning human again?" Killian asked with a mixture of impatience and wariness.

"The deal you made to save your father expired when he died," Gavin explained, addressing John. "That's why you became human again."

"You were there when I woke up," said John. "How did you know where I'd be?"

"I saw your father leaving the cabin after one of his visits and I recognized him; I was a ranger at the park where he had that accident all those years ago. I had always had my own suspicions about his miraculous recovery and he confirmed those for me. So, in turn, I told him what I knew."

"Did that include telling him that his death would lead to me being human again?"

"No," Gavin answered quietly, not flinching away from the anger in John's tone. "I don't know how he figured that piece out. Maybe he just guessed." After a pause, Gavin continued, "He loved you, John. And he was desperate to get you back."

John got up and turned his back on the others, walking over to stare out the large windows that overlooked the

29

lake. Killian checked his watch and saw that there were still twenty-five minutes left in their vigil. It seemed an endless amount of time. Five minutes passed before Gavin spoke again, addressing John.

"Do you see them out there?"

"No," John answered, still facing the windows. His voice was steady enough, but it sounded foggy, like he was developing a cold. "Edmund will be keeping them hidden though. That's part of his job."

"How come I was able to see them yesterday, then?" Killian asked.

"I've been wondering the same thing," said John, turning back toward them. "I think Edmund must have slipped for a second. He had his hands full with me."

"What do you mean?" Gavin asked.

"I didn't exactly want to be there once I realized who our potential victim was," John answered. "It took the whole flock to keep me in line."

Silence fell in the room once again. The next time Killian checked his watch he saw that they only had ten minutes to go. He began to hold out a cautious hope that Sarah would make it.

"Come on," he urged her quietly. "Hang in there, sweetheart. Just for a few more minutes. Please."

He had barely finished speaking when Sarah's breathing hitched once, twice, and then stopped altogether.

"No!" Killian shouted. He lunged forward, but Gavin knocked him aside none too gently and pinned him to the ground.

"Get off me," Killian snarled. "I'd do anything to save her!"

As soon as Killian had spoken those words, his world went dark. He was lost with no point of reference, no sense of time or direction. He couldn't feel Gavin holding him down, or the ground beneath him. Then a voice boomed out, echoing in his brain. That voice was ancient and powerful, and it seemed to come from everywhere and nowhere simultaneously.

"Would you truly do anything to save your wife?"

"What's happening? Where am I?"

"You are inside your own subconscious. Your physical body is right where you left it, lying on the floor in your living room."

"You're one of them, aren't you?" Killian asked, abandoning his fruitless attempts to turn his head. It seemed he no longer had a head to turn. "You're one of the odedaud."

"Yes."

"You killed her?"

"No. She died on her own. Her soul was not strong enough."

Anger coursed through Killian like poison, but he thought better of expressing it.

The voice went on, "You are currently at a crossroads. Your future and that of your wife depend on the road you choose to take. For her to live you must agree to leave her and become one of us. I think you already know most of what that entails."

"And if I say no?" But even as he asked the question his heart burned to say yes.

"Then you wake up just as you were. But no matter what life-saving measures are attempted, you wife will not survive. Save your own human life and you forfeit hers."

31

Killian was quiet for a moment, trying to calm himself and think about the situation logically instead of emotionally.

"She'll still die eventually," he said. "From old age if nothing else. So when that happens…"

"You will be returned to your human body, which will be in precisely the same condition it is in now."

So what John had said was true, although knowing that didn't make Killian's decision any easier. No matter what he chose, he and Sarah would never be together again. If he decided to join the ranks of the odedaud he might at least catch an occasional glimpse of her from far overhead, although that would probably just make the separation more painful. If he went back to his human body now, he would have to live with the knowledge that her death was his fault.

He weighed the pros and cons in his mind for what might have been one minute or twenty. It was hard to distinguish the passage of time in this strange mental limbo.

Then, with a silent prayer that he was doing the right thing, he gave his answer.

Gavin and John stared at one another in silent horror as Killian's body collapsed to the ground. Gavin started to drag him to the couch, but John intervened.

"Leave him where he is. It'll make more sense that way."

"What do you mean?" Gavin demanded.

"We need a plausible story to tell the paramedics when

they get here. And a plausible story to tell Sarah, for that matter."

"Why do you want to call the paramedics in the first place? They'll both be fine, thanks to Killian's deal."

"Yeah, but Sarah doesn't know that," John answered. "And we can't tell her, because she would be in danger if she knew too much. So we have to go along with Killian having some mysterious illness."

"Carbon monoxide leak," Gavin suggested. He lowered Killian gently back to the ground, and then rushed to open windows. "The reason the gas didn't affect us is because Killian opened the windows after he got home, and the place was ventilated well enough by the time we got here. But it wasn't enough to stop him from fainting."

"Works for me," John said, joining in with Gavin. It took them only a short while to open every window in the place. When John got back from propping open the back door, Gavin was staring down at the two bodies on the rug.

"Why isn't she waking up?"

"Sven always gives people the chance to back out of the deal. Didn't he do that when you were with him?"

Instead of answering, Gavin said, "Maybe we should move him behind the sofa or something."

"Why?"

"Better to keep him out of Sarah's immediate line of vision. We don't want her to start panicking when she wakes up."

"There's always a chance that he'll be the one to wake up," John pointed out, but he helped Gavin move Killian's body anyway.

"No," Gavin said grimly. "If I know him half as well as I think I do, he'll go through with it."

"I guess we'll find out soon enough."

Then, they waited to see which prone figure would start to stir.

CHAPTER 4

Sensation came back to Killian all at once when he said yes to the voice inside his mind. His first impression was of being caught in a wind tunnel, with air whooshing around him and buffeting him from all directions. The noise was overwhelming and his whole body felt cramped and tight, like he had curled up into the fetal position without realizing it. Another gust of wind caught him and he instinctively threw his arms out for balance—only to discover that he no longer had arms at all.

Now he had wings.

His eyes, which up to this point had been tightly shut, now flew open in shock, and he instantly regretted it. He had once taken a helicopter ride over a glacier and its surrounding forests. That was the view he was getting now, only this time there was no comforting pane of thick glass between him and the outside world. Even from this high up, however, he could see each individual shingle on his roof, and the breaks between them. He could even see that he needed to clean his gutters.

What a stupid thing to be thinking about right now.

"Got that right," a man said. But he wasn't hearing that voice with his ears. It seemed to be coming from inside his own head.

Killian tried to turn to see the speaker—thinker?—but the simple movement was enough to knock him out of the air current that had been holding him up. He flapped his new wings urgently, feeling ridiculous as he did, and managed to get back up to his previous height. The other birds, five of them, began to circle him. Rather than risk turning and falling out of the sky again, Killian let them pass through his field of vision one by one. He saw one bird with a distinctive white mark on its head. Was that the leader of the flock?

"Guess again," said a different voice, British this time. It definitely wasn't the voice of the one who had turned Killian into an odedaud, but there was still a ring of authority there.

"Very perceptive," said the Brit approvingly, eavesdropping on Killian's thought.

"It's not eavesdropping," came the voice of the one who had turned him into an odedaud. When he spoke the others stopped circling and faced Killian in a line. The largest bird was in the middle, and the one with the white mark on his head was directly on his left as Killian faced him. Leader and second-in-command? Killian thought so.

"My name is Sven," the leader said. "And we are not eavesdropping on your thoughts. How can we help but listen when you're broadcasting so loudly?"

"I didn't know I was. Sir."

"Well now you know better." Sven turned gracefully in the air to face the rest of his flock, turning his back on his new recruit. "Natalie, you will be responsible for our new member's training and orientation. Take him home and answer any questions he has. I expect there will be quite a few."

Four of the five birds in front of Killian flew past, heading east, leaving only the smallest one behind. Killian quickly stifled his feelings of annoyance and embarrassment—of course he had questions. But if any of the others picked up on it, they made no comment.

"They didn't hear you. I blocked you off from them," said a woman's voice inside his head.

"You can do that?"

"Yes. I'll teach you how if you want. It'll definitely make your new life as an odedaud a little easier."

At this mention of his new life, Killian looked down at the remains of his old life. He saw a shadowy figure go back inside from the back deck. What was going on down there?

"John was outside watching us," said Natalie, following Killian's train of thought. "Your wife is coming around now, and your other friend is looking after her."

"And she'll be okay?"

"Yes. It's part of the terms of the deal you made. Even Sven can't break that."

Killian looked down again, lost his balance, and started falling. Natalie swooped down to where he was struggling.

"Don't flap around so much," she told him. "Your feathers will help you keep your balance. That's what they're there for. Just stretch your wings out all the way, like this."

Killian copied her demonstration and immediately felt more at ease. At least until he lost focus for half a second and let one arm—wing, not arm, having arms was a thing of the past—drop a bit. He felt himself turning in that direction, overcorrected, and ended up doing a stupid kind of twirl in midair. Natalie didn't laugh at him, just cuffed his wing with her own and knocked it level again.

She must hate getting stuck with the newbie, he thought, forgetting that Natalie could hear him.

"Actually, training you is a relief," said Natalie. "It gives me an excuse to get away from the rest of them for awhile, and it's nice to have a new voice in my head."

"Do you realize how strange that would sound coming out of a human's mouth?" Killian asked.

"No stranger than it sounds being projected directly from my mind into yours," Natalie shot back, and just like that they were both laughing.

"You seem to be getting the hang of staying in one spot. Want to try some actual flying?"

"Sure." He figured there was no point trying to hide how nervous he was. She moved away and he followed, watching her every move and mimicking her as best he could.

"This will become like second nature to you soon enough," Natalie assured him. "And you don't have to be self-conscious or try to hide your thoughts around me."

"It's not you I'm trying to hide them from," Killian replied.

"You don't have to worry about the others either. They're not listening in on us right now. I'd be able to feel it if they were."

Killian took her word for it. They flew in relative silence for awhile, with Natalie occasionally doling out tips and instructions. Killian found himself actually relaxing a little bit—until he made the mistake of looking down to try and figure out where they were. The sight of the scenery whizzing by made him forget what his wings were supposed to be doing, and he lost almost twenty feet of altitude before he managed to correct the problem and get back up to where Natalie was waiting for him. He felt a quick flash of irritation at himself for making the mistake when he'd been doing pretty well. Or maybe Natalie was the one who was annoyed and he was just picking up on it.

"Like I said before, I'm not annoyed with you. And you're not just doing pretty well, you're doing *really* well. You didn't even need my help to get back up here."

Something in her tone made Killian ask, "Was that a test just now?"

"I prefer to think of it as a... teachable moment. I would have stepped in if it looked like you were in real trouble." They got on the move again and she added, "There's a place coming up in just a few minutes where we can stop for a little while."

It briefly crossed Killian's mind to press on and pretend he wasn't absolutely exhausted. Then he remembered false bravado would be pointless because Natalie could read his mind and know how tired he really was.

"I guess some rest would be nice," he said.

"For the record, I didn't suggest that we stop because I thought you might be tired."

"Why did you suggest it, then?"

"Stopping will give me some time to answer any questions you might have. And I can teach you another lesson."

"Oh yeah? And what's that?"

39

"Landing."

They approached a small copse of birch trees and she talked him through the descent, then made him watch her before he attempted it himself. He stumbled a little when he alit on the branch beside her, but he didn't fall off and tumble to the ground, so that was something. He rested a few minutes, and then turned to Natalie.

"Okay, first question," he said. "What did Sven mean when he said you were in charge of my orientation?"

"Mainly helping you get back to the roost without falling out of the sky. You wouldn't be of much use to the flock if you were roadkill."

"And who are the others in the flock? I've spoken to Sven already, and John mentioned someone named Edmund. Is he the British one?"

"Yes. And you had it right when you guessed he's Sven's second-in-command. They've been flying together for a long time. About a hundred years, I think."

"A hundred years? But I thought you turned human again after the person you saved dies. How is he still around after so long? Or Sven, for that matter?"

"It's complicated."

Killian didn't have to be telepathic to understand that Natalie knew more than she was telling, but he dropped the issue for the time being.

"So there's Sven and Edmund, plus you—who are the other two?"

"Charles and Randall. Charles was the one heckling you just after you turned. Randall's pretty quiet, but when he does talk he's by far the least obnoxious of the bunch. He and Charles are both seekers."

"Seekers?"

Natalie shifted her weight back and forth. But eventually she answered, "They... look for people who are about to die."

Several questions popped into Killian's head, but first and foremost among them was: "Why?"

"Because that's what keeps our powers strong. We sort of harvest their souls for energy."

Killian couldn't form an adequate response in words, but his mind did the work for him, projecting an image of a vampire sucking someone's blood.

"I don't like thinking of it like that, although I guess it's a pretty accurate description," Natalie said, reacting to the picture in his mind. "But like I said, that's what gives us our powers, so we have to do it."

"Who made up that rule anyway? Or the time limit thing?"

"So John mentioned that, too? No wonder Sven was so angry. And in answer to your question, I don't know. Sven says, 'It has been the rule since the beginning.' But I think it has something to do with honor. Like if the person can survive that long on their own it means they have a warrior's spirit, so we can't lay claim to their soul." She paused and then added, "Sven's very big on honor."

It was hard to imagine someone like Sven being honorable when he actively sought out human souls to feast on. Then again, Killian would now be doing exactly the same thing.

"You can be different," Natalie said quietly. "You don't have to enjoy it like the others do."

"How often does this happen?"

"Usually a few times a week. We can go longer than

that between victims if we need to, but Sven likes to eat as often as possible so we can keep our guard up."

"Against what?"

"He won't say."

"And how am I telepathic? I haven't, you know, harvested anyone."

"You're sharing energy with the rest of us. Don't ask me about all the mechanics of it, though, because I've never asked."

There was a stretch of silence, and then Killian said, "I have a lot to learn, don't I?"

"I did too, when I first started. And speaking of learning, I think it's time for your next lesson."

"Which is what?"

"Taking off. We should get going again. If you're ready, that is."

"Sure."

As with the landing, Natalie first explained what to do, and then demonstrated. Killian was much less graceful, but he did okay once they were actually in the air and on the move. He could see himself coming to enjoy this part of his new life. Right now it seemed like the only positive thing in what he knew would be a long, long road ahead.

This caused a new question to occur to him, and he asked, "Sven said my human body wouldn't change or decay. So what's going to happen to it?"

"Doctors will think it's an unexplained coma. You'll stay in the hospital with machines keeping you alive and monitoring your vitals. But you're right, there won't be any physical deterioration. Whenever you become human again you'll look exactly the same as you did when you woke up this morning."

Had he really been human only that morning? It seemed impossible to believe.

"The doctors will certainly be baffled when I wake up. Or do you think John will steal my body and stash it in the cabin where his father kept him?"

"Sorry, but there's no chance of that happening with you. John and your other friend called an ambulance for you, mainly so your wife wouldn't get suspicious. It would have looked weird if she woke up and they told her not to worry about her comatose husband on the floor."

"How do you know they called an ambulance? Or are you just guessing?"

"I've been keeping an eye on things from afar." There was a pause, and for a brief moment Killian's mind was entirely his own again, as Natalie's consciousness went somewhere else. Looking over, he saw that she was still flying a perfectly controlled course, but she seemed to be running on autopilot. Then she was back.

"It looks like the paramedics took your wife as well. Doctors just told her they're keeping her overnight for observation. She's not overly pleased."

"No, I bet she's not," Killian said, and he laughed even though it was hard to be happy he'd sentenced her to a life of not knowing, of always wondering what had happened to him. But he took comfort in the fact that perhaps her worry would not last forever. Maybe she would learn the truth for herself, or maybe she would just move on from him, find someone else to make her happy.

You'd better hope neither of those things happen.

That thought sounded more like Natalie's than Killian's.

43

"Edmund will be impressed with you," said Natalie. "You weren't supposed to hear that."

"Sorry. I didn't mean to snoop or anything."

"It's okay. But forget about it, at least for now. We're getting close, and I won't be able to keep everyone else out. They'll want to see the show."

"What show?" Killian demanded, turning his head to look at her—and promptly losing altitude and his balance. He got himself back on track, and then repeated his question.

"Dinner," Natalie answered. "Normally we just eat berries and seeds and stuff, but they try to find something really gross for your first meal. Part of your orientation."

"Sounds more like hazing to me."

"Call it what you want," said Natalie. "On a positive note, your sense of taste is less refined than it was as a human. And whatever gross food they find, I'll choke it down right alongside you."

"You don't have to do that."

"I know. But John did it for me."

They had been flying over inky black water for a while and now a cliff loomed ahead of them. A cluster of trees on the top were silhouetted against the moon, and Killian's sharp eyes could pick out his new family members standing near the precipice, watching him and Natalie approach. His landing was far from smooth, but he thought it was at least better than his first attempt.

"Is that what took y'all so long? You couldn't make it all the way here without stopping for a break?"

This voice was new, and it had a distinct Southern accent. Killian could only assume it belonged to Randall.

"I saw a teachable moment," Natalie said, shaking out her feathers. "And yes, Killian, that's Randall."

"Welcome to the club," Randall said, twitching his wing in a little wave. "Dinner's just through the trees, by the shore of the pond. Natalie can show you the way."

"Thanks," said Killian, and he followed after Natalie as she walked away.

"You should try hopping rather than walking," she told him, noticing his awkward gait. "But you'll get used to it. And I can see dinner straight ahead."

Killian had been watching his own feet to make sure he didn't trip over them. Now he looked up and saw a small, shallow pond with starlight winking out of its depths. He would have thought it was beautiful if it weren't for the sight of what he was expected to eat tonight. A deer's head was lying by the side of the pool. There was no way a deer could have gotten up here on its own; the flock must have worked together to carry the head back. Still, maybe it wouldn't be that bad. He had eaten venison before and enjoyed it. Then they got closer and he saw that the deer had been dead for several days, if the maggots crawling around in its eyes were anything to judge by. He felt bile rise up in his throat but pushed it back down. He would not give Sven and the others the satisfaction of knowing how disgusted he was.

He hopped forward, Natalie by his side, and used his beak to scissor off a mouthful of meat, working quickly so he wouldn't have to think about it too much. Since he no longer had teeth, he cocked his head back and swallowed it whole, pretending it was medicine. His less refined taste buds helped a little bit, but the texture felt entirely wrong going down his throat. It reminded him of calamari, or raw oysters. Natalie stopped after six bites and Killian took two more, just for good measure.

"What's for dessert?" he asked. He heard quiet laughter, or at least he thought he did. He and Natalie made their way back to the rest of the flock. Sven approached and Killian watched him with apprehension.

But all Sven said was, "You will go with Natalie tomorrow to continue your training. Get some rest; you're going to need it."

Then he flew to the other side of the ledge, where Edmund was. Charles and Randall, who had been watching the exchange closely, went back to thoroughly ignoring both Natalie and the newest member of their flock. The night was quiet, but Killian could still hear a faint whispering in the back of his mind. It was like a TV playing on low volume in the next room over. Curious, he tried to focus in on it and one of the other birds—he couldn't tell if it was Charles or Randall—suddenly flew straight at him. In his haste to get out of the way Killian lost his balance and had to flap his wings frantically to keep from toppling over backwards.

"I'm Charles, for your information," a voice snarled in his mind. "And if I were you, I'd think twice before you try to listen in on private conversations."

"Sorry," Killian said. Hoping he didn't sound too defensive, he added, "I haven't exactly been a telepath for very long. I don't know how everything works yet."

"Maybe you should blame your teacher for that."

"Enough!" came Edmund's voice. There was no real heat to his tone, just annoyance, but it still got Charles to back off. He glided back over to Randall, though he made sure to hit Killian in the face with his outstretched wing as he went. Killian looked around at Natalie, but if Charles' comment had bothered her she didn't let it show.

"I'm not worried about it," she told him. "They always blame me for stuff. I've always assumed it's because I'm the youngest."

"You're not the youngest any more. Maybe they'll lay off of you now that I'm here."

"We'll see." But it sounded like she doubted it. "Get some sleep, Killian. Sven's right, you're going to need your rest before tomorrow."

She turned away from him to face the stars that were visible in front of the ledge. Killian looked in the same direction and for the first time in his life he saw the whole Milky Way spread out before him, with no trees or light pollution to get in the way. The stars that had always captured his imagination looked closer than ever, almost close enough to touch, but he had never wanted so badly to have his feet firmly on the ground. That was impossible without Sarah, though. She was the one who had always kept him balanced. Without her, he just felt lost.

Looking around, he saw that the others were settling in for the night, tucking their heads beneath their wings. He did the same and found it was actually pretty comfortable once he'd gotten used to it. Before he gave in to the physical and mental exhaustion of the day, he spared a moment to wonder what Sarah was thinking about right now, and to wish he could reach out and let her know he was alright.

CHAPTER 5

J ohn watched as his old family flew away, leaving only two birds behind, one of whom seemed to be struggling to stay aloft.

"Take care of him, Nat," he muttered. He was surprised when he got a response.

"I will. And you take care of her."

He turned and went back into the house to find Gavin on his knees with his fingers on Sarah's wrist, checking her pulse.

"Don't try to sit up just yet," Gavin told her. "Just take it easy."

"What happened?"

"Carbon monoxide leak, we think," said John. Sarah twisted her head around at the unfamiliar voice, and then let out a groan. She laid her head back down and covered her face with her hands.

"Sarah?" Gavin asked. "You still with us, honey?"

"Yeah," she muttered, dropping her hands back to her sides. "I guess I shouldn't have turned my head so quickly." She looked up at John and asked, "I'm sorry, who are you?"

It was Gavin who answered. "This is John. He was meeting with me and Killian tonight."

"I also used to be a volunteer EMT," said John, kneeling down beside Gavin. "Do you mind if I ask you a couple of questions?"

"Okay."

"Are you nauseous at all?" John asked.

"No."

"Headache?"

"Not exactly."

"What exactly does 'not exactly' mean?"

"It doesn't hurt, but it feels off. Like I didn't get enough to eat or something."

"Did you eat tonight?"

Yes. Killian and I had Chinese food before he left." Her voice trailed off and she frowned. "Where is he?"

Before John or Gavin could stop her, she had lifted herself up on her elbows and turned her head. Her breathing stopped for a moment, and then quickened.

"Killian?" she whispered, staring at his feet, which were sticking out from behind the sofa. Then she said his name again, louder this time, and turned to look at John. "What's wrong with him? Why won't he answer?"

"Gavin, can you go and get her some water, please?" When Gavin had gone, John told Sarah, "Your husband was unconscious when we arrived, but I've checked him over, too. He's perfectly stable and should be coming around any minute now."

He put his hands on her shoulders, soothing her and at the same time forcing her to lie down again. But her eyes kept darting to the edge of the sofa. Gavin came back with the water and helped Sarah drink a little.

"How did the two of you know to come here?" Sarah asked.

"We were in the room when you called Killian," Gavin answered. "He rushed out to help you. John told me he used to be an EMT so we decided to see if we could be of any assistance."

Sarah nodded vaguely and John noted with some concern that she appeared to be on the verge of fainting again. He made her drink some more water, and then turned to Gavin.

"Maybe we should call an ambulance. Just to be safe."

When the paramedics arrived five minutes later, John and Gavin excused themselves and went out onto the back porch to get out of the way. For a while they looked up at the dark, empty sky in silence. Then Gavin said, "I wonder where Killian is right now?"

Before John could answer, one of the EMTs came out onto the deck.

"We'd like to take both of them to the hospital," he said, "but right now it's the husband I'm concerned about. Do either of you know anything about his medical history?"

"A little," said Gavin, and answered the paramedic's questions as best he could. When the ambulance had left, and Sarah and Killian were on their way to the emergency room, Gavin and John stood in Killian's kitchen in silence.

"We should go to the hospital," said Gavin eventually. "I doubt there's anything we'll be able to do, but it might seem odd to Sarah if she finds out we never even showed up."

"She might think it's weird if I *did* show up," said John, fidgeting as he spoke and not looking at Gavin. "I mean, I'm just a stranger to her."

Gavin studied the younger man without speaking, and he didn't need to be a mind reader to see that John was craving some time to himself. For the first time in a long while, he thought about his own return to humanity—how it had been horribly jarring, but how he had relished the quiet, the lack of other voices in his head. John had hardly had a restful first day back.

"Do you have anywhere you can stay tonight?"

John looked up, saw the understanding in Gavin's eyes, and said, "The only place would be my dad's cabin, but I'm not sure I can go back. There's too much of *him* around there."

Gavin nodded and then said, "I'll drop you at my place on the way to the hospital."

"Thank you," said John, and they walked together back to Gavin's car.

Gavin stayed at his place just long enough to make sure John was settled, and then made the trek down to the hospital, but it turned out to be a waste of time. To quote the doctors, Sarah had had "an extreme negative reaction" upon learning of her husband's condition, so the doctors had given her some medication to help her sleep. When Gavin arrived back home, John was seated at the kitchen table, a stack of opened envelopes in front of him. He looked up when he heard the front door bang shut and then looked quickly away again, but not before Gavin had seen how red his eyes were.

"You don't have to talk if you don't want to," he told John. "But I'll be in my room if you need anything."

John nodded, and Gavin left him to his reading.

～

When Sarah woke the next morning her head felt very foggy—so foggy that it took her a minute to remember where she was or how she had gotten there. The memories that came back as the medication the doctors had given her wore off did nothing to improve her state of mind. Her husband was in a coma, and nobody seemed to have the faintest idea what had caused it. There had been no detectable sign of a carbon monoxide leak at the house, but that was still what her own fainting spell was being attributed to. So the question remained: If she had made a full recovery, why hadn't Killian?

Sarah buried her head in her hands and shut her eyes. There was too much happening too fast, all while she was stuck here in this hospital bed, powerless to do anything about any of it. She felt a hard lump in her throat and swallowed hard, willing it away. Maybe she was alone and afraid, but she would not sit here and wallow in self-pity, not when Killian had it so much worse than she did. She looked up when she heard a soft knock on the door, expecting to see one of the doctors or nurses that kept coming in and out. Instead Gavin and John were standing there. Somehow she managed a smile, and Gavin crossed the short distance between the door and her bed. John hung back, looking unsure of himself.

"We just thought we'd drop by and see how you were feeling tis morning," Gavin said.

"Much better than last night. Still a little out of it, but I'm pretty sure that's from whatever medicine they gave me." Looking over at John, she added, "You can come in, you know."

John's smile still looked a little uneasy, but he took a few steps farther into the room.

"I'm glad you're feeling better. I just wish I could have done more for your husband. The nurse downstairs told us he's in the coma ward?"

Sarah's smile faded at the mention of Killian, and she turned her eyes away, squinting at the far corner of the room instead. "I'm sure you did everything you could." She turned to face her guests again and although her eyes were glistening her voice was stronger—stronger, but still afraid. "Nobody knows what's wrong with him! I think that's what scares me the most about all of this, you know? He was so healthy, and then just out of nowhere…"

She trailed off into silence, her too-bright eyes searching John's face for an answer he couldn't give.

"I'm sure the doctors will figure out what's wrong. Still, I can't even imagine what you must be going through right now. I'm so sorry."

"There's nothing to be sorry for, at least not yet," Sarah replied. "There's still a chance he could wake up."

John was silent, trying to determine if the hope in her voice was real or feigned.

"He *will* wake up," Gavin chimed in when it became clear that John was not going to speak. "Killian's strong, he'll pull through this. And so will you. We'll let you get some rest, but you have my phone number if you think of anything you need."

"Can you do one thing for me?" Sarah asked. Her voice quavered a little on the last word.

"Anything," said Gavin.

"They won't let me go and see Killian. Could you just go by his room and tell him that I'll be there as soon as I can?"

"Of course. Goodbye, Sarah."

"Bye. And thank you. Both of you."

Gavin and John left her room and walked toward the elevators that would take them up to the coma ward.

"I wish we could tell her," John said as they waited for the elevator to arrive.

"You were the one who insisted that we didn't."

"I know. But knowing the truth would at least give her some closure. She wouldn't have to wake up every day with false hope."

Gavin turned and gave him a sharp look. "False hope is better than no hope at all."

"I guess so," John said, but it sounded like he doubted it.

They didn't speak again until they were in Killian's room. If not for all the monitors hooked up to him, he might have been sleeping. Occasionally his eyes would move behind their closed lids, as if he were dreaming, but apart from that he was completely still.

"What are you seeing right now, Killian?" John asked, watching the movement, but he spoke so quietly that Gavin barely heard him. "Where are you?"

CHAPTER 6

A sound like a trumpet blast went through Killian's head, jerking him out of whatever dream he'd been having. His first confused thought was that something must be wrong with him alarm clock, because it didn't normally make this kind of noise. Then the truth of what had happened came flooding back to him. He brought his head out from under the shelter of his wing and saw that he was alone on the cliff ledge except for one other bird. He felt a flicker of amusement that wasn't his own.

"Mornin', newbie." It was Randall's voice.

"There are gentler ways of waking someone up, you know."

"Yeah, but you annoyed Charles last night and he's still in a bad mood this morning, which means I get to listen to him gripe whether I want to or not. He might cheer up if I share this humorous moment with him."

"Glad I can be of service," Killian replied.

"We all have our roles to play," Randall said solemnly. Then he continued in a lighter tone, "For example, I slept in the latest, so I was assigned the role of babysitter. I was supposed to let you wake up on you own, but I got tired of waiting. Everyone else is already at breakfast."

"More venison this morning?" Killian asked.

"Nah, that was just a special treat for you last night."

Randall started to preen his feathers and Killian picked out a band of light red coloration around his beak. That would serve well enough to set him apart from the rest of the flock. This made Killian wonder if he had any distinguishing characteristics of his own.

"Yes!" Randall broke in. "Your distinguishing characteristic is that you never shut up. Did you have ADD when you were a human or something? It's hard to keep up when I'm barely awake myself."

"You could solve that problem real easily if you didn't stick your nose into my thoughts."

"Birds don't have noses."

"Oh you know what I mean. Maybe I can't stop myself from projecting yet, but you can stop yourself from listening."

"True enough," Randall said after a moment of thought. Then he added, "It is kind of weird, though, hearing a new voice. Natalie's been here for about eight years now, and she's the youngest after you."

"When did you join the flock?"

"About twenty years ago."

"And why did you end up here? If you know what I mean."

"That's a question you should never ask," Randall replied, all traces of good humor gone. "Of anyone in this group."

"Okay. Fine."

"Good. Now are you awake enough to fly so we can get something to eat? I'm starving."

They took off and flew over the pond, where the deer's head still lay on the shore. It wasn't a long distance, and Killian thought he did fairly well, watching and copying Randall's every move. The landing was a little rough, but there was no need to worry about embarrassing himself; nobody in the group paid him the slightest bit of attention, with the exception of Natalie, who chirped a greeting before going back to her breakfast. Long before Killian had eaten his fill, Sven ordered everyone to gather around.

"You know your places," he told them all. "Fly, and may we meet safely once more."

Killian was suddenly being buffeted back and forth as the flock took flight. He took off as well but didn't make it very far before someone's wing got tangled with his own —he only narrowly avoided crashing back down to earth. He heard a burst of cruel laughter, but it disappeared from his mind a moment later as Natalie built a mental block around the two of them. With her help he found an air current that buoyed him up and gave his wings a break. As he watched the others soar off in different directions, moving with a grace that seemed effortless, he was both amazed and dismayed at how weak and tired he felt.

"Maybe I should have spent more time lifting weights when I still had arms," he said.

"It wouldn't have made a difference," Natalie replied. "You can think of your wings as arms all you want, but the fact is, they're brand-new muscles. The only thing that will help you get better is practice, so come on."

She flew off and Killian followed.

"I'm sure we'll have plenty of time to work on flying

today," Natalie continued. "And it might be easier without everyone around to pressure you. You'll just be stuck with little old me."

Her tone was a curious mixture of loneliness and contentment.

"You're happier when you're away from them, aren't you?" Killian asked, realizing too late that the question might seem like he was prying.

"You're right, you are prying," said Natalie.

"You don't really feel that way."

"Oh don't I?" Natalie stopped in midair and turned to face him. He almost bumped into her but got his wings positioned in time to use them as brakes. "And just how do you know what I feel?"

"Because..." Killian hesitated, and then plunged on. If he was wrong, she would let him know about it for sure. "Because right now it's like you're proud of me. Not mad, not for real. It feels like you're testing me and you're happy I passed."

"Again, how do you know for sure?" Natalie pressed him, but she didn't deny what he'd said.

"There's an undercurrent. On the surface you say one thing, but I can read how you're really feeling underneath. Is that the odedaud version of body language?"

That made her laugh. "That's one way to look at it, I guess. Were you good at reading people as a human?"

"I don't know. I've never given it much thought. Were you always gifted at teaching?"

"It wasn't just a gift—it was a job. At least it means I get to provide some value to this group."

The contentment was gone from her voice now. The bitterness behind the words was so strong Killian could almost taste it, like he'd just bitten into a lemon wedge. Natalie turned to keep flying and Killian followed.

"Teaching someone the ropes sounds like the most important job of the group to me," Killian told her. "I'm just sorry you're stuck with me as a student."

"I didn't mean it like that," she said, and he sensed her honesty. "I just get lonely sometimes. But you should break the monotony nicely."

"Are you being serious or are you just saying that to try and make me feel better?"

"Why don't you tell me?"

But suddenly that riptide of emotion was gone. Killian broke out from behind her and flew alongside, thinking maybe her eyes would give him a clue. But they were beady and blank, completely unlike human eyes.

"How are you doing that? Can you even hear me right now?"

"Yes, but only because I want to. Guarding your thoughts is pretty easy once you get the hang of it. You just picture a wall and keep part of your mind focused on that and the rest focused on whatever you want to keep hidden."

Killian tried, calling to mind photos he'd seen of the Great Wall of China, but he immediately started to fall when he stopped thinking about the act of flying. As before, Natalie did not swoop in to save him but instead waited while he corrected the problem on his own and ascended back to where she was hovering, her wings outstretched and still.

"Maybe you should concentrate on one thing at a time, at least for now."

It was clear she was trying not to laugh, but Killian

realized that this laughter wasn't meant to be cruel, so it didn't bother him.

"Maybe you're right," he replied. "Where are you taking me to hone my skills anyway?"

"Here," she answered, and sent him a mental picture of a building he recognized all too well.

"We're going *there*?"

"Ouch! So loud with the panic. What's wrong?"

"I'm probably at that hospital right now, or my human body at least. And you said they were keeping Sarah overnight, so what if she's still there? What if she sees me or I see myself?"

"We'll be in some trees near the entrance to the emergency room, so there's virtually no chance of either of those things happening," Natalie soothed him. "Even if you did see your own body there wouldn't be any major consequences. You would just weird yourself out a little."

"And Sarah?"

"She's still in the building," Natalie answered after a beat of silence. "But not in the emergency room. And like I said, we'll be well hidden. Just don't worry about it too much, otherwise you'll make both our heads hurt."

Killian spent the remainder of the flight trying and failing to follow this advice. He focused on the present long enough to land on a tree branch where the thick foliage allowed him and Natalie to see but not be seen. Then he went right back to dwelling on the past. The concerns he'd voiced to Natalie were only part of the reason he didn't want to be here. In reality, this place held a lot of memories for him, memories of the worst experiences of his life. He'd been here countless times as a young boy to visit his father after the man had gotten sick. Twelve years after that, his mother had died of a heart attack in the emergency room here, and Killian had found himself an orphan at eighteen.

Now Sarah would come here and visit him, as he had once come and visited his dying father. He scanned the building's many windows, wondering which one looked into his room, and which looked into Sarah's. Was his wife even now sitting behind one of those panes of glass, perhaps staring at the very tree in which he now perched?

"What exactly is the plan today?" he asked after a long time.

"We're going to watch the ambulances pull up to the entrance and guess whether the patients inside will live or die."

Trying not to think of his mother—and naturally thinking of nothing else—Killian asked, "Does Sven make you do this every day?"

"Yes. But you seem like a good student, so you probably won't be stuck here for long. Sven will have you out there seeking in no time."

"Why doesn't he use you?"

"He did for a while, but most of the potential targets I picked out ended up living. Eventually Sven got tired of me wasting everyone's time and sent me here to 'refine my instincts.' In other words, he wants to keep me out of the way. Now, while we wait for the first ambulance to get here, I want you to clear your mind. You're going to need a lot of mental stamina for this, so don't focus on how tired your new muscles feel, or what a strange and messed-up situation this is, or building a wall to fool me into thinking you're doing what I asked. Try to feel everything around you, not just with your physical senses but with your inner ones as well."

She fell quiet and Killian snuck a peek in her direction. Her eyes were closed and she sat perfectly balanced on the branch with barely a feather stirring.

"So interesting to see yourself through somebody else's eyes," she said.

"Sorry."

"Don't apologize, just pay attention to what you're supposed to be doing."

Killian closed his own eyes and sat still. He felt the rough bark under his talons, and the breeze ruffling the feathers along his back. He felt the minute vibrations caused by a bug crawling on the trunk of their tree, heard the buzz of its wings as it took flight. When he had grounded himself by concentrating on these things, he started to tune in to the rhythm of his breath and his heartbeat. He was surprised at the soothing effect it had. Was this how Sarah felt when she did yoga? If so, it was a pity he had never joined her in the practice, even more so now that he would never get the chance. He wondered what life would be like for him when Sarah eventually died and he regained his humanity. What sort of technological advances would there be sixty or seventy years in the future?

"Hey!" Natalie broke in. "You call that calming your mind?"

"I started off okay," he replied, a little defensively.

"Yes, and then you started thinking about Sarah and all bets were off. Just put her out of your mind, at least for the time being."

"She's my wife!" Killian yelled, making Natalie flinch

back not only from his volume but from the pain he was radiating as well. "It hasn't even been twenty-four hours since I had to let her go, and you think I can stop thinking about her just like that?"

"I'm sorry. Really, I am. I know this can't be easy for you. God knows it wasn't easy for me either when I first started, but the fact is you're making things harder for both of us."

"So shut me out, then."

"I can't! The harder you think about something, the louder you project it. I know you can't control it and you don't mean to, but you're practically screaming about her inside your head right now."

She let him stew over that in silence until the anger and grief baking off of him began to lessen. Then she asked, "Ready to try again?"

Killian responded by shutting his eyes and falling as silent as possible, trying to prove he was a good student. Once again he grounded himself, and then focused on his breathing and his beating heart. Both seemed to be going too fast at first, though they slowed to a calmer pace the longer he sat there. Thoughts of Sarah still drifted across his mind, but he pushed them gently away and didn't let himself get distracted.

"Much better," Natalie told him. "Now open your eyes. The first ambulance is about to pull up."

Her prediction came true less than a minute later.

"How did you know that would happen?"

"I was listening for it while you were clearing your mind. When the back opens you're going to reach out to the patient telepathically."

"How am I supposed to do that?"

63

At that moment, however, the doors of the ambulance opened, and Natalie did not answer. From his vantage point behind the leaves Killian saw that the patient was a young woman with short blond hair. She was covered by a blanket, so he couldn't see what was wrong with her with his physical eyes. Tentatively, and with more than a hint of skepticism, he reached outward, thinking of his mind as an extension of his fingers. He encountered a wall, but not like the one Natalie created. This one was thin and flexible. He could see things moving just on the other side, darting around like a school of fish.

Are those thoughts? Is this what another person's mind looks like?

Gathering his courage, Killian plunged through the barrier—and instantly regretted it. He felt everything the woman was feeling and it overwhelmed him, because he could still feel everything in his own body as well. He was sitting on a tree branch gripping the bark with his talons, but he was also lying on a stretcher with his right leg strapped down and radiating waves of pain. He was looking at the woman on the stretcher from behind the screen of leaves, yet at the same time he was the woman, looking up into the face of the paramedic rolling the stretcher. He could even smell the man's aftershave, the spicy aroma mingling with the woody smell of the tree in which he sat.

It hadn't even been five seconds, but Killian couldn't take any more. He retreated back into his own mind and basked in the cool, silent dark. After some time he looked over to his right and saw Natalie watching him closely. As soon as they made eye contact a feeling of deep concern washed over him and her voice came bleeding through.

"Hey, are you okay? Can you hear me?"

"I can now," he answered. "Why couldn't I hear you before?"

"Because that mental block you just put up was one of the strongest I've ever felt."

"I didn't mean to shut you out, honest. I wasn't even thinking about a wall. It's just... that was a lot to take in. I wanted some peace and quiet." He paused and then added weakly, "I'm pretty sure the patient has a broken leg."

"Yeah, I'm pretty sure you're right about that," Natalie replied, her tone as dry as his was. Then she grew more serious. "I didn't mean for it to be that rough on you, but this is how John taught me."

"You're saying I have to learn from my mistakes?"

"Exactly."

"So what did I do wrong? Did I use too much power?"

"More like you didn't focus your power in the right areas. Your brain basically has two levels: concrete on top, and abstract underneath. You stopped at the concrete stuff and got overwhelmed by it."

"So it would have gotten easier if I had just kept going?"

"It still would have been a lot to take in, but yes." Natalie searched for another metaphor to use, and then said, "Think about jumping into a really cold swimming pool. The cold shocks you at first, but the longer you stay in the less you notice it. Make sense?"

"Kind of," said Killian.

"You should be able to see what I mean with the patient who's about to arrive. Let me guide you this time."

Another ambulance pulled up to the bay, and when the

doors at the back opened Killian saw an elderly man with an oxygen mask over his face and sensors attached to his chest to monitor his heart rate. He appeared to be only halfway conscious. The paramedics were moving a lot faster with him than they had been with the previous patient. Killian felt his consciousness being drawn toward the man, but he did his best to just sit back and let Natalie steer. When he saw the barrier getting closer and closer, he braced himself for pain that never came. Instead, a barrage of quick images went by.

A child was playing catch with someone in their front yard under a sycamore tree.

A smiling young man held the hand of a young woman wearing a white gown and a beaming smile.

A man who was still young but now creeping toward middle age read a book to two young children, who suddenly morphed into adults reading to children of their own.

But underneath these happy images, these memories of a life well lived, there was something dark. Killian's curiosity was piqued and he tried to wriggle free of Natalie's mental grasp on him to get a closer look, but she held him back. Then the man vanished inside the building and Natalie severed the connection. Killian's mind was once again his own.

"So what's your opinion?" Natalie asked. "Is he going to make it?"

Killian barely hesitated. "I think he's going to die. That darkness that I felt…"

"You have good instincts," Natalie told him. "Sven calls that darkness the death streak, and it's exactly what Charles and Randall spend their days seeking out. The thicker and the darker the streak is, the more quickly death will occur."

Recalling what he had felt and seen inside the elderly patient's mind, Killian didn't think the man had very long to live at all. And now that he knew what that darkness actually signified, he didn't understand why he had initially been curious and not afraid. Even now, underneath the fear, a sense of fascination and interest still remained. What did that say about him and his character? He did not voice this concern to Natalie, and out of respect for his privacy she pretended not to have heard it.

Instead, Killian asked, "What would have happened if you hadn't pulled me back when I tried to go closer?"

"It would have been a shock to your system, like how you got overwhelmed by the patient with the broken leg, only much worse. You would have experienced everything he was feeling. And if you were still down in that darkness when he actually died? I don't know for sure if it would have killed you too, but that seems like a pretty safe bet."

"In that case, I guess I should be thanking you." Another thought occurred to him and he asked, "How come I didn't feel any of the physical pain he was in? Were you guarding me from it, or was all of it contained in that darkness down below where we were?"

"No to both of your questions. I was just directing my focus, and therefore yours, on the abstract. We still had to go through the concrete layer to get there, but it was a seamless transition."

They were quiet while they waited for the next ambulance to arrive, and Killian knew he should be trying to keep his mind clear, yet it was almost impossible. Never in his life had he had so much information to digest and process. His thoughts kept coming back to the way that death streak had looked. How thick and dark had Sarah's been last night? And would he have to actually venture down into that darkness to harvest energy from a victim?

"No," Natalie answered when Killian put this question to her. "Sven and Edmund are the ones who actually pull people's souls. They've never explained exactly what happens, and I've never asked. I don't want to know."

"And if someone tries to help the person, Sven and Edmund kill them somehow?"

It was impossible to miss the darkness in his tone of voice and the course of his thoughts, and Natalie shrank back from it.

"Yes," she answered quietly. "They do."

Killian stared straight ahead, not really seeing anything, just trying to clear his mind. Then the wind shifted, the leaves in front of them parted, and Sarah was there, coming around the corner of the building. She must have been waiting for someone, because she kept glancing back over her shoulder. At first Killian thought he was just imagining things. His thoughts had been with his wife, so he had conjured her up. Or it might have been someone who just happened to look like her. Someone who just happened to be carrying the same purse and wearing the same blouse and jeans. Yes, that could be it.

Then she looked up into the tree and their eyes met.

He felt an instant white-hot pain lance through the center of his skull. The intensity was enough to make him cry out, causing several birds in the neighboring tree to take wing in fright. He vaguely noticed Sarah put a hand to her own head down in the parking lot, before the pain blocked out all observation. Then, as suddenly as it had arrived, it was gone. As his awareness returned he instinctively looked around for Sarah, but she was nowhere to be seen.

"A good thing, too," said a British voice inside his mind.

"What was that?" he asked. "Will she be okay?"

"You both will, thanks to me. What were you *thinking*, Natalie? You of all people know the risks of a saved seeing the one who saved them."

Natalie's shame flooded Killian's mind, but it was quickly stifled and replaced with anger.

"I went where Sven ordered me to go. How was I supposed to predict that she would walk around the corner at just the right moment for them to see each other?"

"Well there's nothing that can be done about it now, in any case," said Edmund. "Just get out of there, both of you. Go to another hospital to train, or work on something else entirely, I don't really care what you do. I'll take care of the girl."

"What do you mean, you'll 'take care of her'?" Killian demanded hotly.

"I mean I'm going to keep her safe," he answered, in a far gentler tone than Killian had yet heard from him.

"Safe from what?"

"Ask your teacher," Edmund replied curtly.

Killian waited until he and Natalie were in the air and moving away from the hospital before he said, "What just happened? Explain."

"Part of the sacrifice you make when you become an odedaud is that the person you saved can never see you."

"But why? I mean it's not like she recognized me as her husband. She would have just seen a couple ravens sitting in the tree."

"Doesn't matter," said Natalie, coming in for a landing in the same copse of birch trees where they had rested the night before. "The way it was explained to me, an act of such selflessness forges a unique bond between you and the person you gave up your life to save. Sarah's soul recognized yours and reached out, causing yours to reach out in return. If you spend too long in each other's presence the consequences could be fatal for both of you. Your souls would keep reaching and reaching for one another until they stretched too far to come back."

"So that pain I felt just now was my soul trying to leave my body? Sven failed to mention that risk when he was explaining things to me."

"Yeah, figures he would. It doesn't affect him personally, so why bother bringing it up?" Killian felt her burst of intense dislike for the leader of the flock, and it was a perfect echo for his own feelings. Natalie continued, "But Edmund was right, I should have been more careful. I'm so sorry, Killian."

"It wasn't your fault," he replied.

"I still knew the risks," she said, her head drooping. "Edmund was right about that, too."

Killian caught a whisper of a name—*Seth*—but he knew he hadn't been meant to hear it, so he didn't press her.

Instead, he asked, "What did Edmund mean when he said he was going to keep Sarah safe?"

"He's going to make her forget she saw you today. If

she dwelled on it, she would be putting both of you in danger without even realizing it."

"But she won't forget me completely, will she?"

"No," Natalie said gently. She was quiet and he could sense her searching for the right words. "Until this morning, Sarah thought your soul was inside your comatose body. Now, whether consciously or not, she knows different. *That's* what Edmund is going to make her forget."

"She's lucky," Killian said after a while.

"What do you mean?"

"I mean she doesn't have to live every day knowing what I did—why I'm in a coma."

"Are you saying you regret your decision?"

"No," he answered immediately, although he wasn't being completely honest. "No. But I guess I'm a little jealous of her. Ignorance is bliss, and all that."

Natalie did not reply, and Killian was left to wonder, for the first time but definitely not for the last, if he really had made the right choice. He didn't question whether it was the right thing for Sarah; that had never been in doubt and never would be. He just didn't know if he was strong enough to carry the burden he'd laid upon himself.

On Natalie's advice, Killian mentioned nothing about that day's incident with Sarah when they met back up with the rest of the flock. Instead, he put all his energy into focusing on what he'd learned. But despite his best attempts to ignore them, the nagging doubts remained. He actually found himself looking forward to continuing his lessons the next day, if only because it would be a relief to escape into someone else's head for a while. That night, while choking down some dinner he had little appetite for, the background hum of the others' thoughts was suddenly cut off, making him look around curiously. Then he heard Edmund's voice in his head.

"Go back to eating—give no sign that anything is different." Edmund waited until Killian had done as he asked, and then continued, "Your wife is safe. I just thought you should know."

"Thank you."

"You can thank me by not letting it happen again."

Then he was gone, as suddenly as if he had just hung up the phone. And in a way, Killian thought, that was exactly what he had done.

CHAPTER 7

When Killian's training resumed the following day, they went to a smaller hospital, far away from anybody Killian had known in his human life. It was even harder for him to empty his mind that morning, but he did the best he could, and when the first ambulance of the day pulled up he readied himself to make the leap from his own consciousness into someone else's.

"Just don't dive in too quickly," Natalie reminded him. "And keep your focus on the subliminal, not the concrete."

"Right," Killian replied, remembering his disastrous first attempt yesterday. The patient who emerged from the ambulance this time didn't look like he had anything wrong with him. But when Killian dove in he immediately felt pain in the lower right-hand side of his abdomen. Keeping in mind what Natalie had said, he didn't dwell on the pain, and instead went deeper into the man's mind. The pain faded and Killian looked around with interest at the memories that were now flashing by. It was like being in a room that was walled with television screens, each one playing a different channel.

"Hey!" came Natalie's voice. "Focus, why don't you?"

Startled, Killian looked around and saw her floating beside him, only she was no longer a bird. Instead, she was just a ball of light, yet somehow he still knew it was her. Interesting.

"Yes, fascinating," she commented. "But not what you're supposed to be looking for."

Killian redirected his concentration—they didn't so much leave the memory room as the room simply dissolved around them. Now they were floating in empty space, but it was lit up from below them. Killian wanted to look closer to make sure there was no sign of that streak of darkness, but before he could make a move he felt himself being pulled back into his own head.

"What did you do that for?" he asked Natalie. Then he realized that sensation of being pulled was still there. "It wasn't you."

"No. It's Randall. We have to go, and fast."

She took off, leaving him scrambling to keep up.

"What's the big rush?" Killian asked. "What's happening?"

"That's the call that seekers put out when they find someone who's about to die."

Killian balked at that, and his meager breakfast began to stir in his stomach.

"We're about to go feed on someone?" Unbidden, the image of a vampire rose to the forefront of his mind.

"We have to," Natalie replied, and Killian could sense her distaste not just for the image he was projecting, but for her own words. "And the critical hour doesn't start until everyone's there. If the victim dies before that, there's nothing we can do. That's why we have to hurry. Come on!"

She poured on even more speed and Killian asked no more questions. He had to use all his energy just to keep up with her.

"We're almost there," she announced after about ten minutes.

"How do you know?"

"Because the call that Randall's putting out is like a radar blip in my head. Can't you feel it too?"

But the only thing Killian could feel was that relentless pull. Although, was it his imagination or was that sensation fading just a little bit?

"It's not your imagination. Think of the call like a rubber band. There was more tension when we were farther away, but now that we're getting closer it's not as bad."

"Take off your training hat, Natalie," came Edmund's voice suddenly. "There'll be plenty of time for that later. Right now Sven's getting antsy."

"We're two minutes out," Natalie told him.

"I know," Edmund snapped back.

They made it to the rest of the group in one minute instead of two, Natalie stopping so suddenly that Killian flew right into her. Cold laughter echoed in his head.

"Sorry."

"No worries," she replied. "And why don't you shut up, Charles? You were new at this, too, once upon a time."

"Enough squabbling," said Sven before Charles could

answer back. "Get into formation. Killian, you're behind Natalie."

And so, his first critical hour began. Around and around they flew, high above the ground—but not so high as to prevent Killian from picking out the growing red stain on their victim's bright orange vest. Part of Killian's mind tried to insist that this man was only a potential victim; after all, the hour had only just begun. But the rise and fall of his chest was too shallow and irregular for there to be much hope. He held on for fifteen minutes in what must have been terrible agony, although Killian didn't dare try and duck into his mind to confirm it. Then, as the man took his last struggling breath, Killian felt something pass right through the center of their circle. At first he thought it was just another air current, but it was warm, like sinking into a hot tub. The strange sensation only lingered for a moment, yet after it was gone Killian realized he didn't feel nearly as tired as he had before.

"Back to your stations, everyone," said Sven as though nothing had happened. "The day is still young."

Killian was very quiet as he and Natalie flew back to the hospital, at a much more sedate pace this time. It seemed obvious that the surge of energy was a result of the hunter's death. His life force had somehow passed through their circle and rejuvenated them. That idea frightened Killian, and he was even more afraid of his reaction to it. Witnessing someone's final moments had certainly disturbed him as a human, so why was he now feeling not disturbed but exhilarated?

～

Although Killian was not aware of it, both Sven and Edmund knew exactly what the newest member of the flock was thinking—and they were both pleased with what they found.

Yes, there was definitely potential there.

A week later Killian and Natalie were racing toward another call, the third one since Killian had joined the flock. Natalie was once again setting a furious pace, but Killian was pleased that this time it wasn't nearly as difficult to keep up with her.

"You're getting much better," Natalie told him now, following his train of thought. "Can you feel the radar blip this time?"

He tried, calming his mind and reaching out the way she'd been teaching him, but there was nothing.

"Don't worry about it for now. We're almost there."

Once again, they were the last ones to arrive. They hastened toward the rest of the group to get into formation, but Sven intercepted them.

"Go," he said to Natalie. She obeyed without a word, although Killian felt a flicker of curiosity from her.

Then a strong wall went up around Killian's thoughts and Sven asked, "What is your opinion? Will the woman down there live or die?"

So this was a test, then.

"Yes," Sven replied to the thought Killian had not meant to project. "And the result will determine your role in this group. Now answer me."

Killian closed his eyes and focused on the wind—on

the sound of it and the way it flowed through his feathers, lifting him up. When he was thus 'grounded,' he reached out and felt the human presence in the house below them. She was alone and currently lying in bed, reading a book. There was a box of tissues and a bottle of something that looked like cough syrup on the nightstand to her left. Looking a little deeper, Killian discovered that although she was seeing the words on the pages in front of her, her focus was elsewhere. She was missing somebody: an older gentleman, perhaps her father. Killian caught a brief glimpse of the man in a hospital bed, but shied away before he could get lost in that particular memory. It reminded him too much of his own father, and it wasn't what he was supposed to be looking for anyway. He dove still deeper into their potential victim's mind and found the death streak at last, but it was very faint.

Killian returned to his own mind and opened his eyes to find everyone staring at him. But he spoke only to Sven.

"My instinct says she'll survive. She's sick, laid up in bed, but I don't think it's going to kill her in the next sixty minutes."

"We shall see."

Then the voices of the other were back, like a wave of static on a radio that had slipped out of tune. Killian followed Sven back to the group and got into formation, keeping his mind focused solely on the task at hand to try and conceal where his thoughts truly lay. What had Sven meant when he said Killian's role would be determined by this test? Was this something every new recruit went through?

At the end of the hour the woman in the house below them was still alive, and Sven sent everyone back to their stations. He made no indication of whether Killian had passed or failed his test.

"I know you're curious, Natalie," Killian said as they made their way back to the hospital. "I can sense it."

"Stop," she told him firmly. "That was a serious wall Sven built while you two were talking. Clearly he wanted it to be a private conversation, which means you shouldn't tell me."

"Suit yourself," he replied. But all that afternoon she felt distant from him, putting up a mental wall of her own.

Later that night, back on top of the cliff that served as their home, Sven asked Killian for a private word. They flew off into the trees together, and then Killian once again felt the thick barrier go up, separating the two of them from the rest of the flock. Only then did Sven speak.

"You have progressed admirably in a very short amount of time. In light of this, I have decided that you will join Charles and Randall as a seeker. I trust Natalie has explained their role to you?"

Killian was taken aback by Sven's announcement, but he still managed to answer, "Yes, sir. They seek out people who are about to die."

"Exactly. And with you seeking as well, we will be able to find even more victims."

Killian didn't much care for that term. It made him feel too much like a predator stalking its prey.

"An apt analogy," said Sven, eavesdropping on his thoughts. "For that is exactly what you would be doing."

"Why do we do it though?" asked Killian before he could lose his nerve. "Why do we harvest souls for power? And how long has it been going on?"

79

"Long enough. And we have good reason for keeping up our strength. The time is coming, perhaps sooner than you think, when that reason will be revealed—not just to you but to all of the members of this flock. However, you are not ready to hear it tonight. Not while you still cling to your humanity and allow your conscience to torture you over what needs to be done."

"Last week I *was* human. It's the only life I've ever known."

"I never said it would be easy to give it up. But if you surrender to your animal nature, to the primal instincts buried deep inside you, you will become so much more than you are now. And it will free you from the burden of your human emotions." There was a thoughtful pause, and then he added, "Still, I suppose your empathy may prove to be an asset."

"How so?"

"It makes it easier to reach out. But you must not let your emotions cloud your judgment; you can ask Natalie about the consequences of allowing that to happen. The training for your new role will begin tomorrow. Charles has been seeking for longer than Randall, so he will be your instructor. I suggest you get a good night's rest."

Thus bringing the meeting to an abrupt end, Sven took off, heading away from the cliff where the rest of the flock was gathered. As he stood alone in the trees Killian saw another dark figure fly off in the same direction. Even from this distance he could make out the white mark on the other bird's head.

"What was that all about?" Natalie asked as soon as Killian landed beside her.

"Can we talk alone?" he replied.

"We are," she said after a moment.

"Sven says I'm going to be a seeker. Starting tomorrow."

"So this morning was a test for you?"

"Yeah."

"I thought so. I guess I should have expected it, given how good your skills are." She sounded gloomy and resigned.

"I had a good teacher," he said, trying to cheer her up.

"Thanks. Well, congratulations on the promotion. I should let you get some sleep before your big day tomorrow."

She moved away from him, and when he tried to reach out he found his way blocked by a solid wall. He was surprised how much that hurt, being cut off like that. He made no attempt to connect with Charles or Randall, who were both watching him closely, but instead flew over to the edge of the cliff and stared at the ground far below. He remembered being in an airplane as a kid and loving the idea that he was looking down at a patchwork quilt, the land split up into little squares, each with its own unique texture and color. He would enjoy getting to experience that view every day, instead of just staring at the entrance to the hospital's emergency room. And as little as he liked to admit it, the idea of being able to reach into someone else's mind with his own—to sense their fate when they themselves had no inkling of it—gave him an incredible and heady sense of power.

Natalie was another factor in this whole thing. She was by far the kindest out of the group, and he enjoyed their time together. Maybe a little too much. He felt a hot surge of guilt as he admitted that to himself. Surely Sarah hadn't forgotten about him the way he seemed to be forgetting about her. But why was he agonizing over this? It wasn't like he had a choice in the matter. He tucked his head under his wing to try and get some sleep, wondering if maybe Sven had been right when he said human emotions were a burden.

CHAPTER 8

S arah had definitely not forgotten about her husband. Despite being discharged she still spent nearly all her time at the hospital, sitting with Killian and wondering what to do. According to Killian's doctor, people could linger in comas for a very long time. There were risks associated with that of course but surely it was too early to even start thinking about that. A week wasn't that long. Surely there would be a change soon, either for worse or for better, that would help her decide which course of action to take. She just wished she had some idea of what had caused the problem in the first place, so she would know if there was cause for hope or if keeping him alive was just prolonging his suffering. She had no idea what Killian would have wanted. It wasn't like they had made any sort of plan for this sort of thing—being as young as they were they had thought themselves invincible. And of course there was no way he could tell her now.

Sarah glanced down at her watch and saw it was time

for her to go. She took hold of her husband's hand and raised it to her lips.

"Please tell me I'm making the right call," she murmured into his skin. "And please keep holding on. I love you, baby."

She replaced his hand gently on top of his blanket and left the room. She was thinking back to the night after she had been sent home from the hospital, wishing she could return to that day and do things differently.

Gavin had given her a ride home, and as soon as she stepped inside the house, the quiet and the emptiness seemed to take on physical weight. A bird cried somewhere, breaking the awful silence, but it sounded as lonely as she was. She dropped her purse in the middle of the floor, curled up in Killian's favorite chair, and let herself go to pieces for a while. Afterwards she felt a little better, but it was still too quiet for her to bear. Instead of calling one of her friends or just turning on the TV as background noise, which is what she would have done now if she could turn back time, she picked up the phone and dialed her mother's number. Even looking back on it, she didn't know why. She hadn't spoken to her mother in almost a year, and whenever they did talk they almost always ended up arguing. Still, she figured her mom deserved to know what had happened.

Marissa Black picked up on the second ring.

"Sarah?" she asked in disbelief.

"Hi, Mom."

"What's wrong?"

"Why does something have to be wrong? Maybe I just wanted to hear your voice." Her own voice skipped up and down the register as she spoke, but she shut her eyes tightly, still crunched in a ball in Killian's chair. *You will get yourself under control. You will not break down.*

"You wanting to hear my voice? It would be the first time in quite a while," Marissa said. Then, in a tone so different it might have belonged to someone else entirely, she continued, "I know we don't see eye to eye on much, but you're still my daughter. I know when something's bothering you."

"I'm just a little overwhelmed, I guess."

"Are you pregnant?"

Her mother's matter-of-fact tone shocked Sarah out of her misery, and now her voice trembled with irritation rather than suppressed tears.

"No, Mother, I'm not pregnant. Would I be this upset if I was? I just thought you should know that I wound up in the emergency room last night."

"What?" Marissa asked, shocked. "Why? Did Killian do something to you?"

"Why would you even *think* that?" Sarah demanded, but she shouldn't have been surprised. Marissa had never approved of her daughter's choice for a husband. "He had nothing to do with it. I had a fainting spell, and apparently I was out for a while. The doctors kept me overnight, but I was discharged this morning. I'm at home now."

"Do they know what caused it?"

"They're not completely sure. They thought it was a carbon monoxide leak at first, but firefighters checked the house last night and didn't find any sign of one. I'm supposed to call and set up a follow-up appointment with my doctor."

"Well you make sure you do that as soon as you can, so they can make absolutely sure everything's all right."

"I will."

After a brief pause, Marissa said, "If you don't mind me asking, why didn't my dear son-in-law call and inform me about any of this?"

I do mind you asking, Sarah thought. Out loud she said, "He had a good reason, Mom."

"I knew you would defend him!"

"He's in a coma!" Sarah almost screamed. It felt good to pour some of her own pain out and inflict it on someone else. "Is that a good enough reason for you?"

There was silence on the other end of the line for a long time. Then, finally, Marissa spoke.

"I'm sorry, honey. I shouldn't have jumped to conclusions. I'm sure this must be very hard on you. Did that happen last night as well?"

"Yes. He was unconscious when I came to, but the doctors have no idea why he won't wake up."

"Or if he'll wake up?" Marissa asked quietly, verbalizing the thought that Sarah could not bring herself to say.

"I don't know what I'll do if he doesn't," said Sarah, her eyes beginning to burn once more. "I'd give anything to trade places with him."

"I'm sure you would, dear. But would he do the same for you?"

Sarah's answer was cold and without hesitation. "Yes, he would. We both meant it when we said, 'For better or for worse.' " Without giving Marissa a chance to reply, she rushed on, "I have to go now. The doctors told me to get plenty of rest."

"Of course. Please let me know if there's anything I can do for you. Or… for your husband," she added with obvious reluctance.

"Right. Goodbye, Mom."

That conversation had been five days ago now. A day after that, Marissa had called again and announced that she had purchased a plane ticket and was coming for a visit. She had not indicated how long she would be staying, and Sarah had not asked; she was too taken aback by the fact that now she had yet another thing to deal with because her mother had seen fit to invite herself along. Maybe she had done it from a place of kindness, but Sarah couldn't help thinking she had some sort of ulterior motive and that it had something to do with Killian.

Still, Sarah could hardly tell her mother no, at least not without hearing about it for several years afterward. Driving toward the airport now, Sarah was forced to admit that it would make a nice change just having someone else in the house to talk to. She just wondered how long that enjoyment would last.

Marissa strolled down the corridor that led to the gates, and then the two women hugged, both with big fake smiles on their faces.

"How was your flight?" Sarah asked as they made their way to the baggage claim area.

"Well, customer service isn't what it was back in my day. But it was just a little puddle jumper over from Montana. I don't know why I don't make the trip more often."

Because you can't stand being anywhere near the man who's making your daughter so happy.

"You're welcome to visit any time you'd like. Hopefully next time it will be under better circumstances."

"Yes, of course," Marissa said. "You're looking well,

but you still shouldn't have to be dealing with all of this on your own."

"Right," Sarah mumbled. "Thanks, Mom."

They were spared the necessity of making more small talk when Marissa spotted her bag—a huge, leopard-print monstrosity—and stepped forward to get it. She made a big show of not being able to lift the suitcase because it was *so* heavy and wouldn't *anybody* help an old lady with her luggage? Sarah stood back with her arms folded, watching and struggling not to roll her eyes.

They didn't speak again until they had reached the car and another innocent passerby had been drafted into heaving Marissa's suitcase into the trunk. Then Sarah said, "So I guess you'll want to get settled in at the house? Or we could get a bite to eat if you're hungry."

"Why don't we pick something up and take it back to your place? That way we can catch up more privately."

"Sure, that sounds great," said Sarah. *And there won't be any witnesses if you decide to start telling me how I made the wrong decision moving out here to the middle of nowhere to live in the woods with a park ranger.*

Back at the house Sarah gave Marissa the grand tour— which didn't take very long as it really wasn't that big. Marissa pronounced everything perfect and beautiful, but Sarah could see her frowning at the way the furniture cluttered the living room, and saw her lips purse at the small proportions of the guest room. But when they stepped out onto the back deck to see the lake, Marissa's gasp of delight was genuine. She drank in the scenery while Sarah watched her, a sad smile on her face. She still came out here almost every morning to watch the sunrise, but without Killian there beside her the beauty of the surroundings seemed cold somehow.

"Sarah, did you hear me, dear?"

"What? Sorry, I got distracted."

"I said you certainly picked a nice location."

"The view is what sold us on the place," Sarah replied. Then she decided to change the subject. "We should go inside and eat. Before the food gets cold."

They went into the kitchen and took out the sandwiches and soup they had bought on the way home. They ate half the meal in silence, and then Marissa spoke up out of the blue.

"Maybe we could go and see Killian later this afternoon."

"Together?" Sarah's eyes, initially wide with surprise, now narrowed. "Why?"

"Don't you want to go?" Marissa replied, avoiding Sarah's question with one of her own.

"Of course. I'm just surprised that you want to."

"Well you shouldn't be alone up there with no one to talk to."

"I talk to him," Sarah answered quietly. She was stirring the soup around in her bowl, no longer remotely hungry. "His doctor says it's good for him. Supposedly it can stimulate brain activity and give him a better chance of recovery."

"The conversation must seem a little one sided. And don't look at me that way," Marissa added as Sarah gaped at her, appalled she had the nerve to say such a thing. "Believe it or not, I'm trying to help you."

"How is any of this *helping*?" Sarah demanded, fighting to keep her voice level.

"I don't think you're grasping the seriousness of the situation, dear," said Marissa. She reached out to take one of Sarah's hands as she spoke, using a gentle but firm mother-knows-best sort of tone. "Whether you like it or not, there's a difficult choice ahead of you."

"Don't treat me like a child," Sarah replied, snatching her hand away and using a napkin to dab at the corners of her eyes. "The doctors made things very clear to me. They also made it clear that it's too early to even start thinking of a decision like that. It's only been a week!"

And you've only been here for two hours, she thought but did not say.

"The longer you wait, the more difficult it will be."

Understanding hit Sarah like a blow to the stomach.

"I never realized you hated him so much," she said, and she felt herself trembling all over. "You came all this way to try and encourage me to give up on him. To kill him."

"I do not hate your husband, and I certainly don't want him to die. But I also don't want you to get your hopes up only to be disappointed. You need to be prepared for the worst."

"And you need to stop acting like you're the expert when you don't understand his situation."

"Does anyone have a clear idea of what his situation is? Have his doctors come up with a diagnosis yet?"

"They're waiting for some tests to come back," Sarah answered.

"Maybe we can ask about that when we go this afternoon," said Marissa. She checked her watch. "It's half past twelve right now. When do visiting hours end? Do I have time for a quick shower?"

"We have until five," Sarah answered, speaking to her half-eaten sandwich.

"Well in that case I'd better start getting ready." She got up from the table, carrying her plate, then looked around uncertainly for the trash can.

"I'll take care of it, Mom," said Sarah, getting up as well. She forced herself to smile and went on, "You just go and enjoy your shower."

Marissa smiled back, but Sarah saw no gratitude there, only a self-satisfied smirk. She had trained her daughter well—to put on a fake smile and act like everything was fine even when everything was falling apart. Sarah threw the trash away and wiped down the table. Only when she heard the water running in the shower did she throw the rag down in disgust and storm outside. The brisk autumn air dried the angry tears streaming silently down her face. She hated the choice that she knew lay before her, she hated this whole situation, but she hated her mother more than anything right now. She couldn't believe that Marissa was really trying to twist this situation to her advantage and get rid of the man she had never approved of.

Stop, Sarah told herself firmly. She closed her eyes and let the breeze coming off the lake cool both her temper and her burning cheeks. *You're overreacting and you know it.*

She stood there a while longer, getting herself back together. When she finally went back inside she was much calmer.

Her mother would have been proud of her.

Marissa's 'quick shower' ended up lasting almost forty-five minutes. And then she had to dry and style her hair, re-do her makeup, and change her mind half a dozen times about what she was going to wear. More than once Sarah convinced herself that Marissa was deliberately drawing things out, just to keep her miserable for a little while longer. And more than once she had to remind herself not to let her emotions rule her logic.

It was almost three o'clock by the time they finally got to the hospital. They went up to Killian's room and Sarah, forgetting her mother's existence for the moment, sank into her accustomed place at his bedside and took his hand, stroking the back of it gently with her thumb.

"You have company, Killian," she told him. "Besides me, I mean. My mom's here. She wanted to see how you were doing." Sarah paused, her head cocked to one side, looking for all the world as though she were listening for his reply. Then she said, "You seem pretty strong to me."

It was true; Killian may have been enjoying a Sunday afternoon snooze if not for the feeding tube protruding from his side and all the machines hooked up to him.

"There's another chair, you know," Sarah said now, glancing over her shoulder to where her mother still lingered on the threshold. Marissa came the rest of the way into the room and sat down on Killian's other side.

"It looks like all this equipment is doing a good job of keeping him stable," Marissa said as she settled in.

"Having visitors helps him, too," said Sarah.

"What sort of things do you talk to him about?" Marissa asked

Sarah shrugged. "Just normal stuff. Funny stories, remembering our first date, the way the weather's starting to change. He's always loved this time of year, when the leaves start to fall."

"I've never cared for autumn myself," said Marissa. "Especially not since I've gotten older. Summer's always been my favorite season."

Sarah somehow found it in her heart to feel sorry for her mother, who was clearly out of her element and grasping at straws to start a conversation. So she played along.

"I've always loved summer, too. Probably because it was a break from school. But I can see why he likes this time of year. There's something... I don't know, refreshing about it. Like there's the promise of a new start. I've come to realize that more and more since I moved out here."

Marissa was visibly unsure how to respond to this, so they lapsed into silence once more. Suddenly she said, "And who are you?"

Sarah jumped and followed Marissa's gaze to the door. "John!"

"Yeah. Um... hi," he replied, clearly flustered. "Um... I was just checking to see how Killian was doing."

"There hasn't been any change, so I guess that's good news," Sarah said. "He's hanging in there."

"That's good to hear."

"Excuse me," said Marissa, with a smile that was more suspicious than sweet. "I don't believe we've met. I'm Marissa Black, Killian's mother-in-law."

"Oh, John Delving. It's nice to meet you, ma'am." He stepped forward with his hand extended, but dropped it back to his side when Marissa made no move to shake it.

"And how do you know my daughter and her husband?"

"He's a friend of Gavin, the head ranger at the park," Sarah jumped in. She didn't know exactly what her mother's intentions were, though she knew the question was more than just a friendly line of inquiry. "They both came over to the house the night all of this happened. That was the first time we met."

"I see. So you just invited yourself along to the home of a complete stranger?"

Sarah opened her mouth in shock and anger, but John spoke before she could, and his voice was calm.

"Killian was helping me, so I figured I would try to return the favor if I could. He took a phone call while Gavin and I were meeting with him, then said something was wrong with his wife and rushed out of the room. I used to be a paramedic, so I thought I might be of some use."

"You definitely were, John," Sarah told him. She turned to her mother and added, "He took good care of both me and Killian."

"You seem like a very involved Good Samaritan, checking up on the health of your patients a week later," said Marissa. "It must have been *some* favor he was doing for you."

"It was." With obvious reluctance John elaborated, "My father died at the park earlier this week. Killian was one of the rangers who found him and tried to help. I wanted to thank him for that, and Gavin agreed to set up a meeting."

"I'm very sorry to hear about that," said Marissa, sounding sincere for the first time since John had entered the room.

"Thank you," John replied. Then he cleared his throat

and continued, "Well, I won't take up any more of your time. Enjoy the rest of the afternoon."

The two women said goodbye and watched him slouch out of the room and down the hallway, his hands shoved deep into his pockets and his head bowed.

"I wonder if he was being honest with us," Marissa said.

"Why wouldn't he be?" Sarah asked. "And why were you questioning him like he's some kind of criminal?"

"Don't you think his actions are even the least bit suspicious? Maybe he and this Gavin person did something to Killian."

"You're joking, right?" When Sarah saw that Marissa was not joking in the slightest, she went on, "Mom, the doctors have run so many tests they would have found some sort of evidence if he'd been drugged or something. Besides, even though I don't know John very well, I do know Gavin. He's a good man, and he thinks the world of Killian. He would never do anything to hurt him."

"It still seems like a flimsy story to me. Isn't it a bit far-fetched that his father died just before all this happened?"

"Someone did die at the park the day before. Killian was heartbroken over it. And before he went to the meeting that night, he said it had something to do with the hiker's death. I just never realized exactly what. There's been so much going on, I never thought to ask exactly how John knew Gavin or what they wanted to talk to Killian about."

"Even so—" Marissa began, but Sarah had had enough.

"Just stop! Isn't all of this bad enough without foul

play being involved? Why are you so intent on making everything seem worse than it already is?"

At that moment one of Killian's monitors started beeping rapidly, and Sarah and Marissa found themselves being shunted back to the waiting area while a large group of nurses and doctors invaded the room, checking and rechecking all the machines he was hooked up to. As scared as she was, Sarah still managed to find some inkling of hope in the situation. This was the first change they had seen since he'd been admitted; maybe it was a sign that the man she loved was still in there, fighting to come back.

It took almost half an hour before Dr. Morgan Peters came to get them from the waiting room and led them down a short hallway to her office. Sarah was determined to keep her composure in front of her mother, but the anxiety began to build as soon as Dr. Peters closed the door. Maybe that spike on the monitor wasn't a cause for hope but the exact opposite—maybe it meant Killian was dying. Some of her feelings must have shown on her face, because Dr. Peters slid a box of Kleenex across the desk and gave her an encouraging smile.

"I don't think we need to be too worried about what happened here today," she said.

Sarah felt a great weight slip off her shoulders at this news, but at the same time her hope diminished.

"So there's no chance it could mean he's waking up?"

"I'm afraid not. The fluctuation might have resulted from a dream he was having, but it's more likely it was just a fluke with the monitoring equipment, like the lead to an electrode slipping off. That would make it look like there was a change in his brain activity when really there wasn't."

She paused briefly, cleared her throat, and then continued.

"It's also possible he was reacting to something in his physical surroundings. I don't mean to pry, but was there any tension between the two of you right before the monitor started going off?"

Mother and daughter both shook their heads, neither of them being truthful. But really, Sarah thought, the tension hadn't been any worse than usual.

"In that case it was probably just an equipment malfunction." Dr. Peters smiled at Sarah and added, "Try not to be worried. The fact that his vitals have been this steady is very encouraging."

"But you still have no idea what caused the coma in the first place?" Marissa asked. Her tone managed to be both detached and accusatory at the same time.

"Mother, please don't," said Sarah, but Dr. Peters turned to face Marissa.

"The diagnosis is still unclear, but we should know more after we get the results of this latest set of tests. In the meantime, I'm afraid there's nothing we can do but wait."

She stood up to leave, and Sarah and Marissa followed suit.

"I have to get back to my rounds, but I will say one more thing: keep coming to visit him, as often as you can. It may not seem like it's having an effect, but studies have shown that it does. I'll be sure to let you know when the test results come back."

She led the two women back to the waiting room, and

EMILY DAVIDSON

then went on her way. Sarah wanted to go back and sit with Killian, or at least say goodbye, but Marissa insisted that both Sarah and her husband had had enough excitement for one day. So, after one last wistful glance in his direction, Sarah allowed herself to be steered into the elevator. She silently vowed to come back again tomorrow whether her mother accompanied her or not.

CHAPTER 9

Although the weather that day was cool and clear, the kind of climate that had always invigorated him as a human, today Killian felt nothing but anxiety about the new journey he would be starting. He tried to control himself as they all ate breakfast—he forced himself to eat a lot, as he was sure he would need the energy for his first day of training. Natalie still wasn't talking to him, so Killian watched Charles' demeanor, trying to gauge whether or not Sven had told him he would have company today. Then Charles approached him.

"Sven just told me about your new position. If he gave you the job he must think you're ready for it, so don't expect me to take it easy on you."

"Wouldn't have it any other way."

"Good," Charles replied. As he turned to leave he added in a much louder voice, "And you should really learn to mind your own business, Natalie."

Then he shut himself off and flew back over to Randall.

"He's one to talk, after trying to listen in on our conversation last night," said Natalie, not seeming overly put out by Charles' comment. After a pause she added, "You okay?"

"I'm nervous," he admitted. "I don't know if I'm ready for this."

"You are. And Charles will be a good teacher."

"Not as good as you, I'm sure."

Natalie cheered up a little, but she still seemed withdrawn and a little sad.

"This isn't something I wanted," Killian told her. "I'm going to miss spending so much time with you. But maybe it's for the best."

"Meaning what?" she asked, and Killian felt a wall start to go up between them.

"Meaning it will be safer for both me and Sarah. As long as my human body stays at that hospital she'll keep coming to visit. Maybe she'll move on eventually, but if I know her, that won't happen for a while. And now that I know what could happen if she sees me... I think the farther away from her I am, the better."

"Guess you're right," Natalie replied. But she was hiding that undercurrent of emotion, so he didn't know if she really believed him or if she just wanted to pacify him. Before he could say anything more, Sven called the group to himself.

"You know your places," he told them, just as he did every morning. "Killian, you will be with Charles until further notice. Fly, and may we meet safely once more."

They all rose into the air and Killian followed Charles, regretting that he didn't get to say goodbye to Natalie or find out what was really going on with her. But he didn't have an opportunity to dwell on it, because his new teacher was setting a blistering pace as they flew north-west, chasing their shadows over the water. Killian made no word of complaint, and eventually Charles let the pace slacken off.

"That was your first test," said Charles. "Glad to see you can keep up."

"Thanks. So where are we going?"

"Right now our territory is split in half," Charles explained. "I search the northwest section and Randall searches the southeast. We're headed to the outermost edge of my section to see how far inward you can throw your mind."

"Right," said Killian, trying to pretend he understood what that meant. Then he remembered pretending was useless thanks to the flock's telepathic connection.

"Yes, it is useless," said Charles, proving the point. "But you'll see what I mean when we get to the boundary."

"What happens if we go beyond the borders of our territory?"

"Can't. The rules forbid it, and even if we broke that rule and went farther afield it wouldn't do us any good. The mental link gets harder to maintain with distance, so we wouldn't be able to send out a call to Sven and Edmund and the others if we found a potential meal."

"Why don't Sven and Edmund look for victims as well? Seems like it would be easier to find someone if they had more sets of eyes looking."

"I believe that's where *you* come in," Charles answered with dry sarcasm. "Sven and Edmund have more impor-tant things to do with their time. I've never been informed exactly what those things are, but you're welcome to ask them directly if you'd like."

"I think I'll pass," Killian replied, matching Charles' tone.

"Smart boy."

Nothing more was said as they flew farther and farther away from the cliff that served as their home. Then Killian noticed that the landscape passing below them was starting to look familiar.

"That's Masonic Point," he said, looking toward the rocky peak looming ever larger in front of them.

"So that's what it's called," Charles replied with mild interest.

"Yeah. It's part of the park where I worked while I was a human."

"Maybe you'll see some of your old coworkers, then," said Charles, coming in to land right at the very top of the peak. "Not that they would recognize you."

The wind was fierce up here, but their feathers kept them comfortable enough. Despite the weather, there were a fair number of early-morning hikers out here, many with binoculars slung about their neck. They had probably come to watch the migrating flocks of geese; he and Sarah had done that once. The noise had been unbelievable, but the beauty of the experience had left a lasting impression. It suddenly occurred to him that they were awfully exposed up here, in plain view of all the hikers and birdwatchers below.

"Glad to see you've dragged your mind out of the past and back into the present," came Charles' voice. "And we're not exposed at all. Those people down there would only see two ravens, nothing unusual about that. Besides, watch this."

He spread his wings, rose high into the air, and performed a complicated series of flips and pirouettes, all while squawking his head off. Doing everything he could not to laugh, Killian looked down and saw that none of the park patrons were paying him the slightest bit of attention. Charles laded again and readjusted his feathers.

"Edmund has a unique talent for shielding us from other people's sight when we don't act like normal ravens. Mostly when we're circling our prey and waiting for them to die."

"I appreciate your confidence in my abilities, but my job is hard enough without you taking pointless risks," came Edmund's voice, making Killian jump. "Stop showing off and get back to work."

"Sorry, boss," Charles replied.

"And don't call me that."

It was only when Edmund had gone that Killian realized he could barely hear any of the others either. But he guessed that made sense given what Charles had just told him about distance playing a factor in their telepathy. Randall's voice in particular was little more than a whisper, so Killian guessed he was the farthest away.

"Very good," said Charles, sounding impressed in spite of himself. "So tell me: is he southeast or southwest of our position?"

Killian focused more intently on Randall's voice and it grew a little louder and clearer. He could now hear the country song that was currently stuck in Randall's head, but he wasn't sure how to tell the direction the voice was coming from. Then he remembered what Natalie had told him, about the call activating a sort of radar blip, and he pictured a radar screen. The image he conjured looked like something out of an old action movie that took place on a ship or submarine: a set of green concentric circles and a wide swath of green light sweeping around it. In what would be the northwest quadrant he saw two dots, which he figured must be himself and Charles. Sven and Edmund must be the two in the middle. Slightly south of them was another single dot, but that must have been Natalie; it was too close to be Randall. That only left the one that was...

"Southeast. He's to the southeast," Killian said, letting go of the image. He was surprised at how exhausted it made him, even holding on to it for so short a time.

"Correct," said Charles. "And while I like the old-fashioned radar theme, you waste mental energy by maintaining a picture with that much detail. Try something else, like this."

The world in front of Killian's eyes vanished and he found himself looking at a simple compass with the same flashing dots he had seen on his own map, but the dots on this one were each labeled with the first letter of their names. Then the whole compass vanished from view and Killian was staring at Charles again.

"How did you label each one like that?

Charles took some time before answering the question, and Killian could sense him figuring out the best way to explain it.

Eventually he said, "Everyone you've ever met is unique, right? Even identical twins have something that sets them apart from one another. Our mental signatures are the same way. You've only known us for about a week, so I wouldn't expect you to be able to identify everyone that way. But there may be something else you can try. First pull up your map."

Killian did so, trying to think of just a compass but unable to get the radar image entirely out of his mind. What he ended up with reminded him of an area map in a video game. No dots were on it except his own.

"Well, it's an improvement," said Charles. "Now keep seeing the map with your eyes and listen for the others at the same time."

Killian did as he was told, reaching out for Charles' first because he knew where his teacher was.

"Nope." Killian's map went dark as Charles hid it from his view. "That's cheating. Don't focus on anyone in particular just yet. You have to realize someone exists before you try to label them."

So Killian tried again, and this time he managed to populate the map with relative ease. He could even see the little dots moving around as they went about their appointed tasks. But there were still no labels.

"That's the next step," Charles told him. "Focus your vision on one particular dot, and then direct your listening that way as well."

"How do I split my attention like that?"

"You're doing it right now with me. Seeing one thing and hearing something from a different direction."

Killian switched focus from listening to watching his map, and a label popped up above Charles' dot. But as soon as he went to move on to the next member of the flock the label melted away.

"You're trying too hard," Charles told him. You need to see the map and hear the voices at the same time, not put more focus on one task versus the other. Multitask."

"I was never very good at that when I was human."

"You're not human anymore," said Charles coldly, and Killian dropped the map from his mind as he turned to stare at his mentor, irritation coursing through him. Charles looked back at him, unperturbed.

"I'm just telling the truth. If you accept that it would be easier on you."

Killian was forcefully reminded of his conversation with Sven the night before, and he gave the same response he had given then.

"My humanity is still too close. Like you said, I've only been at this for a week."

"And as I also said, Sven gave you this position, so he must have thought you were ready for it. In my experience his instincts are usually correct—Natalie being the exception."

"She's the reason I've come so far in such a short time. She's a good teacher."

"Would you prefer to go back to her, then? I'm sure Sven could arrange for that to happen, but I don't think he'd be very happy about it."

Killian didn't answer. He would miss Natalie's company, there was no question about that, but he couldn't deny that he was curious about how far his new powers could stretch. He said none of these things out loud, but Charles was clearly following the train of his thoughts and seemed satisfied.

"Ready to try again?"

Killian brought up his map once more and let himself settle into the background noise in his brain. Then he "zoomed in" on the dot next to his own with both his eyes and his ears. Charles' voice got louder, and the other voices became muted. Zooming back out to look at the map as a whole, he was pleased to see that Charles' label stayed in place. Next, he focused on the dot that was farthest away from them and heard Randall's voice, as clearly as though Randall were standing right next to them. He was still thinking about the same song.

"Howdy, Killian. Enjoying your first day of training?"

Killian tried to reply, but found himself unable to do so. It was taking all the mental fortitude he had to keep his map in place. So he left Randall's head, pulled back, and then focused on the next three dots one at a time, until he had identified them all.

"Well done. Now give yourself a break. It's tough to stay that focused for so long, particularly considering your lack of experience."

Killian gladly did as Charles suggested and saw the world around him once more.

"When did it start snowing?" he asked, surprised to see the little white flurries drifting through the air around them.

"When you were listening to Randall's soundtrack," Charles answered, sounding amused. "He's always humming that stupid song. Eventually you'll learn how to keep part of your mind focused on the map and part of it focused on your physical surroundings. How do you feel?"

"Tired," Killian admitted. "And I haven't even done any real work. You do all this while you're on the move?"

"I do more than just keep a map in my head. I also have to look for our next victim."

The thought of that made Killian even more mentally exhausted than he already was.

"Don't worry," said Charles. "We're staying right here for today. Sven told me he doesn't expect me to do any actual seeking since I'm busy training you. It is nice to have a break."

"Happy to be of service," Killian replied in a dry tone.

They sat in silence for a while, Charles letting his student rest and absorb what he'd learned so far. Then Killian pulled up his mental map again. It was much easier to populate this time, but something was off.

"Where's Natalie?" he asked. He turned his head as he spoke, trying to see both the real Charles and the blinking dot that represented him. The image kept flickering back and forth, but it was still an improvement over what he'd had before.

"What do you mean?" Charles asked. "I can see her just fine."

Killian's map was replaced by Charles' more simplistic version, and he did see a dot not too far south of them labeled with the letter "N." But even as he bent his concentration toward it, the dot vanished from view.

"I think I see what's going on here," said Charles, pulling back from Killian's head. "She's blocking you—not the rest of us, just you specifically. You two have a little lover's quarrel or something?"

"She is not my lover," Killian snapped. He was so focused on being angry that he lost his map again and could only see the gently falling snow and the bird sitting next to him, looking back with beady eyes that betrayed no human emotion. "My lover's walking around on two human legs somewhere down there."

The anger evaporated and longing filled his heart. He couldn't help himself, even though he knew that Charles was getting all of this, too. He built up a wall of his own, deciding he wanted to keep his thoughts to himself.

"Fine," Charles said, sounding impatient. "But Edmund keeps checking in on us to see how your training is going, and he might not like the fact that you're shutting me out. So get your mind back in a good place and let's get back to work."

Still fuming, Killian closed his eyes. He took a few breaths, grounding himself like Natalie had taught him. When he opened his eyes again he was pleased to find that he was seeing his physical surroundings but his map was down on the lower left-hand side of his peripheral vision, where it would usually be in a video game.

"I never would have figured you as the video game type," said Charles.

"I'm not. But my friend Rick kept trying to convert me."

"Whatever works for you, I guess. Now it's time for the part of your training that actually matters. When you were at the hospital with Natalie, did you ever sense anyone who was actually about to die?"

"Yes."

"Remember that dark streak in their mind? What it felt like?"

Again, Killian answered in the affirmative.

"That's what you're going to look for now," Charles told him. "I already sense one streak, but I want you to tell me where it is."

"So we are going to be doing actual seeking today?"

"Look for yourself and find out."

Killian reached out, still keeping the map in the periphery of his mental vision. He thought of the old man from his very first day with Natalie, remembered the dark vein that had so intrigued him as it ran below the memories on the surface. As he bent his memory toward it, he saw another dot pop up on the map, and this one was white while the others were green. Killian cast his mind in that direction but was unable to sense anything about the person it actually belonged to. Exhausted, he pulled back to find Charles watching him intently.

"Well?"

"The person's east of us, just inside the perimeter."

"And?"

"I'm sure you can sense the answer already," Killian snapped back. Fatigue and frustration were making him irritable.

"Humor me."

"I can't tell any more than that. Whoever this person is, they're too far away."

"The person is a she, and distance isn't the issue. She's closer than anyone else in the flock and you were able to sense them just fine."

"Because I already know their voices. I already have a connection with them."

"That does make it easier," Charles conceded. "But you had to put some effort into hearing their voices in the first place, didn't you? Try again."

Killian obeyed and pulled up his mental map. Once again, the white dot appeared as he remembered the death streak he had previously sensed. But this time he stopped focusing on that streak when the dot appeared and just zoomed in on the dot itself, the way he'd done with the rest of the flock. Now he was able to "see" that magical barrier between his thought and another's. He dipped below the barrier and felt a surge of energy rush through him. He soaked it in for a moment, and then looked through the eyes of the woman whose mind he was sharing.

She was sitting in the entrance of a tent, facing a man who was sleeping inside. Her mind simultaneously identified the man as "Ray" and "husband." Killian dove deeper, looking for that streak. It was there, but it was very faint. He wanted to stay longer in the woman's mind instead of going back to his own tired body, but a sharp mental tug called him back to himself. With little choice in the matter, he opened his physical eyes to see Charles watching him intently again. Was that fear Killian felt coming off of him? Or something else? Something like envy? Then the waves of emotion were walled off and he only had access to Charles' words.

"I guess you know a little more about our potential victim."

"That dark streak in her mind is there, but she's not in danger of dying any time soon—certainly not in the next hour." Unable to resist the urge to show off a little he added, "She's on a camping trip with her husband, Ray."

"So tell me: if you know all of that, why could you tell me nothing the first time you tried?"

The answer came to Killian after several moments of thought. "Because I was focusing on the wrong thing. I was still looking for the streak instead of the dot—I mean, the person—associated with it."

"Exactly. It's a mistake that can quickly exhaust you."

As Charles said this, Killian was struck by another realization. "I don't feel anywhere near as tired as I did before."

111

"I thought that might be the case," Charles replied. "But I don't think the same can be said of Ray's wife."

"What do you mean? Did I do something to hurt her?"

Charles was quiet for a moment as Killian tried to fight off the light fluttering of dawning panic. Then Charles spoke.

"Relax. I just checked in on her, she's okay. She's already forgotten about her little moment of lightheadedness. Either that or Edmund made her forget, one of the two."

"And I was the cause of that?" Killian asked, disgusted with himself. "How?"

"That little boost of energy you got came from her. It's one of the side effects of taking a joy ride inside somebody else's head. Normally the humans don't notice anything, but the longer you spend in someone's mind, the more energy you drain from them. And you spent a relatively long time exploring."

"Why didn't you tell me that before?" Killian knew he was now a supernaturally powerful being, but in that moment he felt like little more than a parasite, sucking the life out of an unwitting and unwilling host.

"Like I said, it's not usually a cause for concern," Charles answered him. "Also, considering you haven't been an odedaud very long, I didn't expect you to be able to do that from this distance. Either you have a natural gift, or Natalie is a much better teacher than I gave her credit for. Probably not the latter, though."

Before Killian could decide if that was meant as a compliment to him or an insult to Natalie, Sven's voice echoed in his mind. Judging by the sudden change in his posture, Charles was hearing it, too.

"I see you're doing well with your training, Killian. Here is a new test for you. Randall believes he has found the next soul for us to harvest. See if he's right."

Killian closed his eyes, grounded himself, and cast his mind out to their south, close to the place where Randall's dot was on his map. He found the death streak quickly and focused in on the person it belonged to. Diving through the barrier once more, he found himself inside the head of a man who identified himself as Martin. Unlike the memories he had experienced previously, the ones flashing through Martin's mind had a strange, blurred quality to them. They would sharpen temporarily, and then fall out of focus again. Interesting, but not what he was here for. Floating on the surface of those flickering memories, he looked down and saw the darkness, huge and terrifying. He drew back almost at once; he didn't know what might be lurking inside that abyss, but he knew he didn't want to find out.

"I think he's going to die," he told Sven, once he was back inside his own head. Sven made no reply, but the call went through Killian's head a few seconds later.

"So much for staying in one place today," said Charles, and he took off, not looking back to see if his student was keeping up. They made short work of the distance and arrived at the same time as Edmund and Sven. Natalie joined them less than a minute later. They began their circling and Killian chanced a look down at the ground.

His first thought was that he had definitely been right about the man's fate. Even a non-telepathic human with minimal medical training would have been able to tell he was in serious trouble. They were circling above a two-story house, with a ladder leaning against one corner; it

EMILY DAVIDSON

looked like Martin had been cleaning the gutters when he slipped and fell to the ground. Blood was spreading in a pool around his head, and Killian guessed that the head injury was what had caused the blurry memories. He was glad he hadn't spent more time examining Martin's recollections, or watching him die would be even harder than it already was.

Within minutes of their arrival a car pulled up in the driveway and a woman got out. She saw the ladder with nobody on it and shook her head, but it didn't seem as if she was worried. More like she was half exasperated and half amused that Martin had neglected to put the ladder away after finishing his work. The woman got a few bags of groceries out of the back seat and started toward the front door. Only then did she look toward the ground and see the man—her husband?—lying there on the scarlet grass. She let out a high-pitched scream and dropped the bags of food. Then she raced to the corner of the house, fell to her knees beside Martin, and stretched out two trembling fingers to check his pulse.

She'll only feel it for a second, Killian thought. *Only for a second and then it will be gone, just like that.*

"We all know how this works, we don't need you narrating it for us," Charles grumbled from behind him. Evidently Killian had been broadcasting his thoughts without realizing it.

Down on the ground, the woman's hand made contact with Martin's neck. Sven and Edmund left their places and went into the middle of their circle, and both of their voices vanished from Killian's mind. It wasn't like they were concealed behind a mental barrier, though; they were

114

completely gone. His curiosity was piqued, but Charles recalled his attention to the present.

"Keep the circle closed. Nothing else concerns you right now."

His tone brooked no argument, and Killian sped up to fly just behind Natalie, closing the gap made by Edmund's departure. But he kept looking into the center, where Sven and Edmund were hovering. He knew they were killing the man on the ground, but how? Maybe he could find out if he dipped inside Martin's head.

"No!" said Natalie, Charles, and Randall together. Charles' voice was a sharp command; the other two sounded concerned and a little frightened. One of them— Killian guessed it was Charles—held him locked inside his own mind, unable to hear anyone's thoughts except his own. It was like being human again, and he was surprised at how little he enjoyed that sensation.

Then the hold on his mind was relinquished, just in time for him to feel that weird rush of warmth as Martin died. The woman with him was now attempting CPR, but Killian knew it was a futile effort. He tried to focus on the positives of the situation, like how they all been strengthened as Martin's life force slipped through their circle. Then he felt a wave of disappointment, and it took a few moments to realize that not all of it was coming from himself. He tried to reach out to Natalie, to explain himself, but the wall she had built against him was impenetrable. Sven sent them all back to their stations, and all Killian could do was watch Natalie's silent retreat before finally turning the other way and following Charles back to Masonic Point.

"Why did you stop me from going inside that man's head?" he asked as they flew.

"To save your life," Charles answered bluntly. Then he explained, "That rush you feel after the victim dies—that's their memories, their feelings, everything that made them who they were parting ways with their bodies. I don't know exactly what Sven and Edmund do to make that happen, but if you were inside of the victim's mind and they didn't know it, you would be caught up in the rush. We'd drink in your energy and your life force without even realizing it."

An image filled Killian's mind: a boat being carried irresistibly forward on a tidal wave rushing toward a rocky beach.

"Exactly," Charles said, sharing Killian's vision. "You're the boat in that scenario."

"I guess I should be thanking you, then," said Killian after a long pause.

"I didn't do it for your sake—I just didn't think Sven would be too happy with me if I lost him his star rookie."

They flew the rest of the way back in silence, Killian pondering what Charles had said.

CHAPTER 10

M arissa heaved a deep sigh and shifted in her chair. Sarah, who had been on the edge of dozing off, looked across at her.

"You don't have to be here, you know. I never asked you to come."

They were once again seated on opposite sides of Killian's hospital bed. It was the first time they had been back since Marissa's first day there, and the only reason they were here now was because Sarah had pushed for it, reminding her mother of what Dr. Peters had said about the positive impact it could have on Killian's recovery.

"I was just hoping we could spend some time together," Marissa said, a pouty look on her face. "It is my last night here, after all."

And tomorrow can't come soon enough, Sarah thought.

Out loud she said, "We've been 'spending time together' for almost a week now."

This was a true-enough statement; Marissa kept insisting that the two of them should enjoy some everyday things. Maybe she was acting from a place of kindness, trying to get her daughter's mind on the mundane and distract her for a little while, but Sarah found it more annoying than anything else. Some of their little shopping excursions and lunches out had been nice, but Sarah couldn't help thinking she would have enjoyed herself a lot more hiking along the trails Killian knew so well, with him by her side. And now ever her time with him here at the hospital was made less enjoyable by Marissa's reluctant presence.

"I thought I raised you better than this," Marissa said now, in that guilt-tripping, disappointed-mother tone Sarah hated so much. "I dropped everything and came all the way out here just to support you in this. Do you know how many people would sell their soul to have parents like that?"

"You raised me to be independent," said Sarah. "I don't need you. I can handle this on my own."

"But you shouldn't have to. And I'm very proud of you for the way you're dealing with the situation, but, if I can be honest, I also think you're being foolish."

"Don't be honest, then," Sarah snapped, her voice and temper both rising. "Nothing you say is going to change my mind, so you might as well save your breath."

"You're getting your hopes up too high," Marissa went on, undeterred. "I've told you this from the beginning."

"And I've told you from the beginning that it's not your choice to make. I'm the one with the power to make decisions about his health, and I'm choosing to keep believing in him."

"I just think—"

"Oh, shut up!" Sarah shouted at her, knowing she

sounded like a child but past the point of caring. "Just get out of here! You're not helping me at all, you're making things so much worse."

And she dug her car keys out of her purse and threw them at her mother, whose mouth was open in shock and anger. For a moment, there was complete silence except for the beep and hiss of the monitoring equipment.

Then Marissa picked up the keys from the floor where they had landed and said, with a failed attempt at dignity, "Well, I can see I've overstayed my welcome. I believe I'll stay in a hotel tonight and find my own way to get to the airport tomorrow morning."

"Fine," said Sarah. "Have a safe trip."

Marissa stormed out of the room. Sarah waited until the sound of her heels clacking on the linoleum had faded away before standing up to leave herself; she didn't want her own pain to impact Killian. It didn't matter to her that she didn't have her car; home was about five miles away, but she'd hiked longer distances than that before. The walk would do her good, and it would give her mother time to clear out of the house. She was so distracted as she went down the hall that she almost walked right into someone. She glanced up, muttered an apology, then did a double take.

"John?"

"Yeah. Hi."

"I didn't realize you were still in town."

"I needed my dad's medical records to wrap a few things up. I figured since I was here I might as well swing by and thank Killian for everything he did. I never got the chance last week, before all this happened."

"Right," said Sarah, only half her mind on the conversation. "Well, you know where his room is so feel free. You'll have to excuse me, though. I can't be here any more right now."

"What's wrong?" he asked.

"My mother is what's wrong," Sarah replied hotly.

"Would it help to talk about it?"

Sarah looked up in surprise. The question had come out of nowhere, and Marissa's words rose unbidden in her mind: *You don't think his actions are the least bit suspicious?*

Then Sarah pushed aside her mother's voice and said, "Maybe it would. Or maybe it would help to talk about literally anything else."

"Have you eaten anything yet? We could grab something in the cafeteria."

Sarah bit her lip, hesitating. But John seemed sincere. And they were both hurting; maybe they could help one another heal.

"Sure," she told him. "Just let me go and sign out real quick. I forgot to do it earlier."

She walked away from him, wondering just what she was getting herself into.

A week after Sarah had bade a not-so-fond farewell to her mother, Killian was out seeking on his own, and it was almost as wonderful as being back on the ground, ranging through miles of unchecked forest. Only now the forest was spread out underneath him, the occasional glimpse of frozen blue-white water breaking up the different shades of green and brown. Even more than the spectacular aerial view, he enjoyed the fact that, for the most part, he only had his thoughts for company. The distance made the noise from the others little more than a background hum.

He was flying back toward their roost. The day had not gone particularly well—no victims to be had— but they had fed two days before, so they were still strong. Sven wasn't too worried about it, or if he was he was hiding his thoughts well. Killian felt no urge to go and check; he preferred to remain out of his boss's mind and notice as much as possible.

"A wise decision," said Edmund, making Killian momentarily lose his balance in the air as he twitched in surprise.

"How do you sneak up on people like that?" he asked, half irritated and half curious.

"I wasn't sneaking—you just weren't paying attention. Sven asked me to inform you that you will not be flying back to the roost just yet."

"And where will I be going instead?" Killian asked, caught off guard but trying to hide it.

"To the place where I am now. Find me."

Killian obligingly focused on his mental map, casting around for Edmund's mental signature. He found it with relative ease, but then it vanished, and he realized this must be another test. What would be waiting for him when he managed to reach his destination? He flew on in the general direction of the place where Edmund had disappeared and consulted his map once more, this time pouring more effort into listening for the other bird's thoughts than looking for the dot marking his location. The search didn't get him anywhere, so he was stymied for a moment. Then he thought of a new tactic: maybe he didn't have to find Edmund at all, just the mental fortress he had built to hide behind. So instead of looking for something that was there, he looked for a dark hole.

"There you are," he muttered after a minute or so, locating Edmund's defensive block and heading in that direction. When he got closer he looked again and saw that Edmund had moved a few miles southwest of where he'd been before. Killian altered his course accordingly, but this time he did not let go of the image he held in his mind. He saw Edmund change direction again and he increased his own speed to cut the other bird off.

"All right, you pass," said Edmund as Killian caught sight of him at last, in one of the highest branches of a tree. "Now come down. Sven is waiting for you."

"Why?" He hadn't done anything wrong, at least to his knowledge, yet he still felt like he was being sent to the principal's office.

"You'll see," Edmund replied with a ripple of amusement.

Killian followed him down to the forest floor and saw Sven at the base of one of the trees, dipping his beak into a small pool of water. He looked up as Killian and Edmund approached.

"Good evening," he began, in a very formal tone. "We have called you here to tell you that both of us are highly pleased with the progress you have made in so short a time. We believe you have earned the opportunity to advance even further.

"As you know, Edmund and I are the ones responsible for claiming the lives of those victims who fail to prove themselves worthy of survival. We hope you will accept our offer to join this inner circle."

Whatever Killian had expected from this meeting, it

definitely wasn't that. Several questions popped into his head, and he had to take a moment to collect himself and decide what to ask first.

"What exactly would that entail?"

"I would still be responsible for tracking the group's whereabouts while they hunt, and sending out the summons when one of the seekers finds a victim," Sven answered him. "And Edmund would still be in charge of keeping everyone in line and protecting us from unfriendly eyes. You would help to relieve the burden on both of us."

So Killian would be in the top tier of the group as a whole, but still at the bottom of that specific tier.

"How would I relieve the burden? By assisting you with the jobs you already have?"

"No. Should you accept our offer, you would use your exceptional talent to assess the situation from afar when one of the other seekers believes they have found our next victim. I will send out the summons to the rest of the flock, but only if you believe it would be worth our while to go."

"Which means I would have to accept the consequences if I made the wrong decision."

"Naturally."

"I still don't understand how that would help you."

"If we fly after victims that end up surviving, we waste valuable time and energy," Edmund explained. "You would help us conserve our strength for when we really need it: when someone on the ground interferes and we are forced to capture a soul while the victim still clings to life."

"What about when you take someone's life away, or

their soul or whatever… Would I have a part in that as well?"

He felt a wall go up in his head while Sven and Edmund traded glances. It was an impenetrable force, but it was only there for a moment.

"That remains to be seen," said Sven. "And it doesn't happen very often."

He had a point. Since Killian had joined the flock it had only been done that one time with Martin, the man who had fallen off the ladder.

"You still remember his name?" Edmund asked, sounding surprised.

"I would advise against trying to keep our victims' name in your memory," said Sven before Killian could respond. "Doing that only makes things harder. If merely witnessing a death is painful to you, it calls into question whether or not you can handle being the one who brings about the death."

"Keep in mind," Edmund chimed in, "if you do play a role in the act, you would be helping the victim as well as us. They would die more quickly and with less pain."

That made Killian feel marginally better, but he still wondered if he would really be able to stomach the situation if it ever arose.

"We realize this is an enormous decision to make," said Sven, "and it would be unfair to ask you to choose quickly. Therefore we will give you three days completely on your own. You are free to go wherever you want, but it is our recommendation that you fly beyond the flock's borders."

"I thought that wasn't allowed."

"This is the exception which proves the rule. Putting

yourself out of our mental reach will ensure your privacy, which in turn will ensure that whatever choice you make is yours and yours alone, free from the influence of others. That also means you will not fly with the other seekers, and you will not be summoned if we find a potential soul."

"Tomorrow morning you will leave us when the others fly," said Edmund. "You will speak of this to nobody. And one final piece of advice: once made, your decision is final. There can be no going back and changing your mind."

"Understood."

Killian prepared to take off, but Sven stopped him with a word.

"If you do choose to join our inner circle, you belong to us and only us. There will be no broadcasting your thoughts and feelings to the rest of the flock. We will help you build a wall that never comes down—a place where you can see but not be seen, hear but not be heard. It can be a lonely existence, but that is the price of great power. Now go. You are dismissed."

Killian barely noticed where he was going as he flew back to the cliff top that served as their home. His fellow odedaud all looked up at him as he approached, and he felt their curiosity about why he was returning late and alone, but he built up a thick mental barricade to prevent any questions. Randall and Charles went back to their own conversation, but Natalie approached him and flapped her wings to get his attention.

"Did you hear a word I just said?" she asked when he peeked out from behind his wall.

"No, sorry."

"I asked what happened to make you come back so late? We were all worried about you."

"Don't include us in this, Natalie," Charles said, but he made no effort to shut them out; he was clearly curious in spite of the front he put up. Killian extended his mental barrier to include Natalie, and she added her own power to it.

"Nice to have some privacy," Killian said.

"So where were you?" Natalie asked. "You dropped off the map completely, almost like you'd flown across our borders."

"I had a meeting with Sven and Edmund."

"About what?"

When he didn't answer he felt curiosity and disappointment rolling off of her in equal measure.

"Would you tell Charles and Randall if they were the ones to ask you?"

"No!" Killian answered hotly. "Why would you even think that?"

"They're your new buddies now, aren't they? Now that you've moved on from spending time with me?"

"We spend time together every night. And Charles and Randall aren't my buddies—my coworkers, maybe, but you're the only friend I've ever had in this group."

"So why won't you talk to me?"

"Because Sven and Edmund told me not to. It's nothing personal, Natalie."

"Right. I'll leave you to your thoughts, then."

And then she was gone. Killian, Charles, and Randall all watched as she flew off by herself, heading toward the lakeshore where Killian had eaten his first meal as an odedaud. Randall looked back and made eye contact with

Killian, but Killian did not lower his mental block, so Randall looked away after a few seconds. Killian continued to watch him, thinking. Those two birds over there might not be his fellow seekers for much longer. This didn't bother him very much; he had always felt like the outsider of their group. Losing Natalie was a different story. He hadn't been lying when he said she was the only one he considered a friend. She could have just taught him the basics of being an odedaud and left it at that, but she had gone beyond just being his mentor and really made an effort to make him feel welcome. Now he was potentially setting himself up to have only Edmund and Sven for company for the rest of his time as an odedaud. It was not an inviting prospect.

But he had three days to decide, and he was too wrapped up in emotions to be clear-headed about it tonight. He thought it would be better in the long run to wait until tomorrow to start working through everything. Aching and confused, he put his head under his wing, but sleep was a long time in coming that night.

CHAPTER 11

The next morning, Sven made no fanfare about the orders he had given Killian—he didn't even tell the rest of the flock they would be one member short for the next few days. So Killian flew off in the direction he normally went—and then kept right on flying. As he got close to the edge of their territory he pulled up his mental map, watching the boundary creep closer and closer. As soon as he was across that invisible line, the others vanished, and silence—true silence for the first time in recent memory—flooded over him. Looking down, he saw acres of forest spread out below him, with not a trace of human influence in sight.

He pressed onward, and the same pros and cons he'd been thinking of last night began to chase each other around his mind again. There was also guilt about the way he'd ended things with Natalie last night. Whatever he decided, he didn't want to leave off that way; she deserved better, even if it meant disobeying Sven and Edmund. He tried to reach inside the boundary from where he was, but it didn't work. So he flew back to the border, making sure he was well cloaked before he crossed over again. He found Natalie and sent a message to her: not words, not even a picture. Just a ping. He ducked outside the boundary, waited a minute or so, and then ducked back in and sent a second ping.

"Killian?" came the response, just the faintest whisper.

He sent her a picture of where he was; there was an abandoned hunting cabin below him that would serve as a handy landmark. Then he flitted back over to the other side of the border. When he checked a few minutes later she was much closer to him. Soon he could see her with his physical eyes, a dark shape bobbing along in the air currents above him. He sent another ping to get her attention, and they both swooped down to land on the roof of the cabin.

"What's going on? Why are we meeting all the way out here?"

He made sure they were concealed before he answered her. "I'm not supposed to be inside our borders. Sven and Edmund told me to leave and spend some time to myself."

"Why?" She caught Killian's hesitation and said, "Right. You can't tell me."

"I just came to say I was sorry about last night. It really wasn't anything personal."

"Right. Well, thanks for the apology," she said. "But if there's nothing else you're allowed to tell me..."

"You're that eager to get back to the hospital?" Killian asked, taken aback and a little hurt at her abrupt desire to end the conversation. Then he sensed the answer and said, "You're not. There's just something else on your mind."

"It's nothing you should worry about," she said, not looking at him. But he caught the name in her head nevertheless.

"Why are you thinking about Sarah? Is she okay?"

"Yes," Natalie hastened to reassure him. "You'd know if she wasn't. It's just... I saw her at the hospital earlier today."

"And?"

"She was with John. And... the thing is..."

"Spit it out, Natalie!"

"John had his arm wrapped around Sarah's shoulders. And she seemed perfectly okay with it being there."

Killian was unable to speak, overwhelmed as he was by confusion. Why would Sarah let John into her life in the first place? The two of them had been visiting him, so clearly Sarah was still keeping the faith. Although it was possible they hadn't been visiting him at all. Maybe they had gone to see somebody else. But then why go together?

"They went up to your room," Natalie said, following his train of thought. "That's where they were when you called me."

John knew Killian's situation, so that might explain why he was visiting the hospital every so often. But it didn't answer the question of why he was doing that with Sarah. Unless he was just pretending to like her, to have an excuse to keep visiting Killian without making Sarah suspicious?

"Why would you even tell me about this?" Killian snapped suddenly at Natalie, his mixed emotions bursting out as anger.

"Because you deserve to know what will happen if... if she loses her faith in you."

Killian didn't want to hear it, and he knew it would only make the decision in front of him that much more difficult, but how could he not listen to what Natalie had to say?

"What happens?"

"There's no going back to your human body," Natalie told him. "Ever. Because you'll have nothing to go back to."

"You mean I'll be stuck as an odedaud for the rest of eternity?"

"Yes. You'll watch your friends and family live and die, you'll watch the world change, and you'll have to live with the knowledge that you'll never really be part of it again."

As Natalie painted the vivid image Killian felt the deepest, purest pain he had ever experienced. It was only much later that he realized not all of that pain had been coming from him. He had been right about one thing: this was going to make his choice a lot harder. He suddenly remembered that Natalie could hear everything going on inside his mind and, with an effort, turned his thoughts in another direction.

"I'm sorry," Natalie said. Then she added, "Come on, we should go. Or Sven will be pissed."

"Go where?" Killian asked as she prepared to take flight.

"What do you mean where? Didn't you feel the summons just now?"

"Sven thinks I'm beyond our borders, remember? He didn't call me. But you should get going. I'll see you later, Natalie."

Without giving her a chance to reply he turned away from her, took off, and crossed back over the border. He flew with no sense of purpose or direction for what felt like at least an hour. Being on the move had always helped him as a human, and it seemed this was also true in his bird form. Then he abruptly turned and headed back the direction he had come. There was no way he could make his choice without knowing where he stood with Sarah, and with John. Hot jealousy surged through him at the mere thought of John's name, but he did his best to calm his mind and search out the person he wanted to find. He located John easily enough; he was driving along a back road near the group's western border. If he kept up his current direction and pace he would cross over at about the same time that Killian got there.

As he flew, Killian thought about how they were going to communicate. He knew John was able to receive thoughts, if not to send them; Killian's last night as a human was proof of that. Would John understand what was happening if he suddenly heard a whisper deep inside his mind, maybe accompanied by a brief spell of dizziness? That could be bad if he was still behind the wheel of the car.

Checking in on the location of his prey once more, Killian saw that John had turned off the main stretch of road to the edge of a meadow, and he wasn't alone. Sarah was in the car with him. It seemed the two of them had decided to go on a romantic picnic after visiting him in the hospital.

Jealousy spurred him on at a reckless pace, but he slowed as he got closer, remembering the potentially disastrous consequences if Sarah were to see him. He hid himself high up in a tree, a perfect place to watch but not be seen. They were eating sandwiches and drinking sodas, sitting in the bed of a pickup truck— but not Killian's truck. John must have gotten his hands on one. It was difficult to hear what they were saying from this distance, and he didn't dare try to go into either one of their minds. It would have been dangerous for Sarah, and John might realize that someone was eavesdropping.

Then he noticed the cattle dog that was roaming around, occasionally lifting its leg against something. Killian didn't know whether it was possible to occupy another animal's mind in the same way he could occupy a human's, but it was worth a try. So he made sure he was well hidden in his tree, and then left his own body behind. He suddenly found himself not with two legs but with four, and with short, coarse hair in place of feathers. His vision was no longer sharp and defined, but blurred shades of gray. The hearing was fantastic, however, and the sense of smell almost overwhelmingly so. The dog he was now occupying thought of itself as "Ziggy" and thought of John as "New Daddy." Killian made Ziggy lie down in the grass and put his snout on his paws, using the dog's ears to listen in on the conversation between John and Sarah.

"You have no idea what you've done for me since... since that night," Sarah was saying. Just hearing her voice was enough to make Killian's heart ache so fiercely he was sure it would break. "But I shouldn't even be here right now! I should be sitting beside him. What if he wakes up and there's nobody there? Or what if he... what if he slips away? After what happened this morning, I don't know what to think anymore."

"Staying in that hospital room day in and day out is

going to do nothing for your own wellbeing. Killian's doctor will call you right away if anything changes."

"You sound like my mother. The whole time she was here she kept coming up with ways to keep me from going back."

"I'm not saying don't go back. But you have to take care of yourself, too. That way you can take care of him when he wakes up."

"I want to keep believing that he's going to be alright, but it's getting harder every day," Sarah said, tears forming in her eyes now. "Maybe Mom was right. Maybe I'm getting my hopes up too high."

John wrapped an arm around her shoulders, though Killian could see that he looked scared. He knew what would happen if Sarah decided to let Killian go.

Please don't let that happen, John. I don't want to be stuck like this forever.

John glanced around at the trees. It might have been a random action, or he might have been looking for a certain bird. Then, before Killian quite knew what as happening, Sarah had hopped down from the bed of the truck, crossed the meadow, and knelt in front of him. She reached out a hand and started playing with Ziggy's ears. Knowing it wouldn't be proper dog-like behavior to just get up and leave, Killian sat there and endured her touch. He tried to savor it, but it hurt to be this close to her, see her in pain, and not be able to say a word. A few gentle licks to her palm was the closest he could get to returning her affection.

"I just wish I knew what he wanted," said Sarah, speaking to John but looking at the dog. "He's the one who should have the most say in the decision, but he can't say anything."

"Did you ever talk about it with him?" There was a cautious curiosity in John's voice.

"No," Sarah answered, turning as he approached. "We both thought nothing could touch us."

Killian couldn't take any more. He retreated back into his own mind, then took off, heading farther outside the group's borders. He was going northeast but had no more direction than that; he just wanted to get as far away from John and Sarah as possible. This decision was already the hardest one he had ever had to make, so why did he keep finding ways to make it harder for himself?

It doesn't have to be this hard, a part of his mind whispered. *You already know how to make it easier.*

Yes, Killian thought, *I do know how to make things easier.* He landed high up in a pine tree and watched the sun setting without really seeing it. The sky was fully dark by the time his mind was made up.

It was time to take Sven's advice. He would free himself from this human pain and achieve his full potential.

CHAPTER 12

I n his dreams that night, Killian was soaring alone far above the earth. He didn't know where he was, but it definitely wasn't Oregon—not with the snow-capped mountain range off to the west. He was heading for a large tree in the distance. He knew that if he made it there he would have all the answers he sought. Before he got anywhere close though, he heard Sven's call in his mind. He tried to resist the summons, but his wings seemed to have taken on a life of their own, turning toward the radar blip going off in his head.

He joined the formation impossibly quickly, but they had only just started circling when the others vanished and Killian was alone with the figure on the ground below; he could barely make out the form through the thick trees. Curiosity got the better of him, and he flew down through the canopy of leaves to get a better look.

He wished he hadn't.

It was his friend and fellow ranger Rick who was lying there. It didn't look like he was breathing but Killian hoped that was just his eyes playing tricks on him. If he had died, why had that mysterious force not passed through their circle? He ghosted a little lower on silent wings and confirmed that Rick was still alive; Killian could see the gentle rise and fall of his chest. Then Rick opened eyes that were not their normal shade of green, but beady and black. They stared straight through Killian and he jerked back in surprise.

He woke up before he could fall out of the hollow tree where he was spending the night, but it was a close thing. He stared out at the star-strewn sky, the moon making everything seem bright as day, and tried to calm himself down. It was just a stupid nightmare, after all. Nothing to be scared of. But the dream had brought to mind something he hadn't considered. What if one of their victims was someone he knew? The idea of killing a stranger was abhorrent enough, but helping to kill someone he knew and liked? Killian wasn't sure if his conscience would let him do that.

Killian closed his eyes again and tried to relax. It took a while, but eventually he managed to fall back asleep. He once again found himself flying alone above a forest. This time he recognized it as the one on their flock's border. The dream demanded that he look down, and that was when he saw the human figure below him, glimpsed between breaks in the cover of the trees. It took a moment before Killian realized what was so strange about what he was seeing: the man was matching his speed. But that was impossible. Up here there were no obstacles to navigate, and down on the ground there would be roots and branches, maybe even trees that had fallen and blocked the path. And even if there weren't, how could a human run as fast as a bird in flight? Looking ahead, Killian saw another break in the foliage. When he got there, he put on the brakes and stopped, hovering in midair with his wings outstretched. On the ground the man who had been keeping pace with him stopped as well.

Killian spiraled down, landing on a low branch of a tree that had been split in half by a lightning strike. He was now just above the eye level of the man on the ground, who appeared to be in his mid-thirties. He wasn't even breathing heavily, despite the enormous amount of energy it must have taken to keep up with Killian. He stood with his head bowed, the setting sun shining in his dark gold hair. Tentatively, Killian reached out with his mind. When he felt the mental block that was built against him, he knew who he was dealing with.

Edmund raised his eyes at last and smiled.

"Hello, Killian. We need to talk."

But before Edmund could say another word, Killian snapped awake again, feeling frustrated and disappointed. Then his more pressing concerns rose to the forefront of his mind: like the fact that he was now on the second of his three days and was seriously doubting the decision he'd made the night before. He stretched his wings and flew toward a river he had passed the day before, hoping to find some fish to eat for breakfast. He couldn't help but glance down at the ground as he went. Of course there wasn't anyone down there, matching his speed or other-wise. But the landscape was exactly the same—Killian realized he was in almost the precise location that he'd seen in his second dream from last night.

All thought of breakfast forgotten, he got his bearings and then put himself on the same path he had followed in his dream. Soon he came to the clearing where Edmund had stopped. He knew it was the right place because the lightning-struck tree was there.

And there's only one tree that's ever been struck by lightning? part of his mind inquired. He ignored that voice and alit on one of the tree's uppermost branches, allowing him a view of the whole clearing.

"Hello, Killian," came Edmund's voice. "We need to talk."

Exactly the same words as from the dream last night, but this time it was no dream. Killian looked around, trying to hide his surprise.

"Where are you?" he asked. Then he pulled up his mental map to try and answer his own question.

"That won't do you any good," Edmund told him. "I'm hiding myself from Sven—he wouldn't like it if he knew I was here, and that's an understatement. Stay where you are, I'll come to you."

He was gone without giving Killian a chance to reply. Moments later, though it seemed like much longer than that to Killian, Edmund landed beside him in the tree.

"What happened to leaving me on my own for three days?" asked Killian.

"It was always my plan for us to meet out of Sven's earshot. That's why I convinced him it would be best if you went beyond our borders."

"And why did you want to meet me in the first place?"

"It's... difficult to know where to begin."

Edmund fell silent and Killian caught a strange image: a disembodied human hand holding several playing cards, shuffling them around. It took him a moment to realize that he was watching Edmund put his thoughts in order.

"Did John tell you his theory about Sven using his father's death to punish him?"

"Yes, he did," Killian answered, wondering where this conversation was going.

"I agree with him. It seems highly unlikely that Ryan Delving would somehow discover he could turn John human again by taking his own life."

A shiver that had nothing to do with cold wind squirmed its way through Killian's body.

"I thought Ryan fell from the top of that ravine. Are you saying he jumped?"

"More like Sven pushed him," Edmund replied sourly. "He planted the idea in Ryan's head, and then forced John to watch as Ryan acted on it."

"Why did he want John out of the way so badly? And why not just kill him outright?"

His cool, matter-of-fact tone surprised even him. The scene he had witnessed yesterday was still clanging around in his head, but he did his best to quiet the echoes so Edmund wouldn't hear; that was something he wanted to keep private.

"John, like myself, was coming to doubt Sven's leadership and morals. He made the mistake of voicing those feelings. In answer to your second question, if Sven had just killed John, that would have destroyed the flock; they wouldn't follow a murderer. So the only way to get John out of the picture while keeping the rest of the group together was to take away his power and make him human again."

There was a long pause before Edmund continued, "I also have a theory about Sarah."

"I already know Sven is the one who hurt her," said

Killian. "And according to John, he had every right to do that, because there was a risk for exposure."

"Then why did he go after her and not you?"

Killian could think of no answer to that. He was amazed the question hadn't occurred to him before now.

"My theory is that Sven *wanted* you to become an odedaud, so he attacked the one person he was betting you'd save." Edmund paused, collecting his thoughts again as he tried to explain himself. Then he went on, "You saw us while you were still human, and I know you've wondered how that was possible. At first I thought it was merely an error on my part; it took everything I had to keep John in check once he realized what was going on. But now I believe Sven took down my wall because he wanted you to see us. He sensed your abilities before you were turned, and he wanted you curious enough to start poking around."

"Ryan saw you, too," said Killian, suddenly remembering.

"What?" Edmund asked him sharply.

"He said something about how the odedaud were here. At the time I thought his head injury was just making him talk nonsense, but now…"

"Maybe Sven made Ryan speak, just to give you something to go on," Edmund said, finishing Killian's thought.

Killian's head was reeling as he struggled to grasp the implications of what Edmund was saying.

"Why did he want me so badly in the first place?" he asked eventually. "You guys were doing just fine before I came along."

"I don't know why he wanted you specifically, but he certainly doesn't want to lose you. I have been in Sven's flock for a very long time, and I have seen several members come and go. You are one of the most highly gifted odedaud I've ever met, Killian, and I'm not the only one who's noticed. Sven may have other plans for you besides just being part of our inner circle."

"And what might those plans be?" Killian asked. He was getting impatient at the vague answers.

"I'm not purposely being vague. It's just that I honestly don't know exactly what he has in mind. But there is someone else who should be able to answer your questions."

"Who?"

"His name is Mir—he's the leader of another flock of odedaud."

"So there are more of us out there?" Killian asked after he had wrapped his head around this latest revelation. "How many?"

"There's just the one flock, at least to my knowledge, and there are only four birds," answered Edmund. "Sven's plan has something to do with an object in Mir's territory; an object Sven covets. With each new member added to the flock, his boundaries extend a fraction farther, meaning there are more souls within his grasp and more opportunities for him to increase his power. That's why he constantly has us out there seeking souls—not just to reap but to turn, the way he turned you. He thinks that with your talents he will be powerful enough to make an attack against Mir."

"Why are you telling me all of this?"

"Sven and I asked you to choose whether or not to become part of the upper echelon of our group," Edmund said. "Now I'm asking you what you will choose to do with the information you'll gain from your new position."

The truth dawned on Killian like a great wave rolling over him.

"You're kidding, right?" he said with a nervous laugh. "You want me to double cross him?"

"Understand, Killian, that I would not ask you to make this decision lightly, but I believe there is no other choice. Sven has grown dangerous and power hungry in the last several years, and I believe you are the only one with the ability to stop him."

"I want more information before I choose," said Killian after some time.

"Such as?"

"Such as what I'd be fighting for. What is it that Sven wants?"

"I told you, I don't know; it's safer that way. He holds more leverage over you than he does over me, but I would still be in danger if Sven found out what I knew."

"Leverage? What sort of leverage does he have over me?"

"Sarah," Edmund said shortly. "He killed John's father to get John out of the way. With you, he wants to do the opposite. If you say no to his offer, or if he thinks you are being disloyal to him, he will not hesitate to try and twist her mind to his own advantage. You know what happens if she dies, but do you know what happens if she decides you would be better off dead than with machines keeping you alive?"

"I stay like this forever." Killian paused, and then asked, "Do you really think he would go that far?"

"Yes," Edmund answered immediately. "I followed

Sven for years without question. I doubted him a few times before the incident with John's father, but that was what cemented my decision to turn against him. Somehow Mir sensed that and reached out to me."

"So you're a double agent."

"I suppose you could call me that, yes."

"How do I know Sarah will be safe from Sven's influence? It seems to me that saying yes to you puts her in more danger than if I just said yes to Sven."

"John's looking out for her," Edmund told him. "At my request. I reached out to him after Mir reached out to me. He's doing everything he can to convince her to keep the faith."

Jealousy washed over Killian once again, but it was tempered now that he understood the circumstances. He was silent for a long while, weighing the pros and cons in his mind.

"I want to help," he said eventually. "But I don't know how I'm going to keep this hidden from Sven."

"Mir would teach you how to defend your thoughts, and I would guard them for you in the meantime," said Edmund. "He's standing by right now, ready and willing to teach you. If you want me to take you to him, we should get going. Sven will get suspicious if I'm away too long."

They flew in silence, and eventually Edmund circled down to a riverbank, where Killian saw a lone raven sitting on the shore.

"Hello, Killian," said a new voice within his mind. Like Sven, it sounded immeasurably ancient, but it also sounded immeasurably more kind.

"Thank you for offering your assistance," said Mir.

"And thank you for offering to help train me."

"Of course. I'd like to fly to a place that is closer to my territory; it will be safer for both of us, and I am stronger when I am near my own borders."

"Could I have a private word with Edmund before we go?" Killian asked.

"Of course," Mir answered, and his presence left both of their minds.

"Why do you think I'm the only one who can stop Sven?" Killian asked bluntly. "For that matter, why does Sven sense so much potential in me? I don't see how my abilities are any greater than anyone else's in the flock."

"It is my hope that Mir will help you to find that answer within yourself," said Edmund. "We will meet back here tomorrow, but until then, you're in capable hands. Good luck!"

CHAPTER 13

Killian was quiet as they travelled east across Oregon. According to Mir, it would take them about four hours to reach the halfway point between the two groups' territories.

"We could go even closer to my land, but that would leave less time for training," Mir had explained.

It would be after nightfall when they arrived. In the meantime, Killian was left to wonder and worry: about whether he had made the right choice, and about Sarah's safety. He had no doubt that his choice to turn against Sven was just, but would he be able to pull it off? About two hours into the journey, he finally worked up the nerve to pose the question to Mir.

"Do you really think I can do this?"

"Yes."

But Killian thought the answer came a little too quickly to be completely genuine.

"I'm not just telling you what you want to hear," Mir

told him. "I wouldn't have asked for your help if I didn't think you were ready."

"But how can I be ready? How do people—ordinary people, I mean—even go about preparing to betray their—"

He broke off. That word he was about to use—was that really the most accurate way to describe whom he was betraying?

"In my experience, first impressions should not be ignored," said Mir. "They may not always be entirely reliable, but I find there is usually a nugget of truth in them just the same."

"So clearly you know the word I thought of just now."

"Yes, but I'm still going to make you say it."

"Why?"

"Because right now your thoughts and emotions are a tangled web, and your true potential is being held captive inside. The best way to untangle the web is by talking."

"Were you a psychologist when you were a human?"

Mir did not reply, clearly sensing that Killian was only putting off the inevitable.

"Family," Killian relented at last. "How do people prepare to betray their family?"

"You dislike the word family."

"Yes. But whether I like it or not, Sven's flock is my family now, or at least the closest thing to it."

"What do you mean, 'the closest thing to it'?" Mir prompted him, in that gentle but demanding way he had.

"I spend all my time with them. We help each other get by and survive. I share my thoughts and feelings with them. But they're not like a human family."

"Why not?"

"For one thing, I don't have much of a choice when it comes to sharing things with them. And…" He hesitated and then went on anyway, knowing Mir would insist upon it. "And with one possible exception, I don't think any of them really care about me. Just about what I can do for them."

"There are some human families like that. People feel like they don't fit, like they aren't loved. But there is always love there, even if it's buried so deeply it rarely, if ever, sees the light of day."

"So Sven cares for me? For everyone in the flock? We're not just pawns in the chess match he's playing against you?"

Mir was quiet for so long Killian didn't think he would get an answer. But Mir eventually spoke.

"I have known Sven for a very long time. He has always believed strongly in honor, and he has always respected those who show it, like you and the rest of his flock. Sven feels a certain bond with people like you, and that bond is all the stronger because those who show honor are so rare in your human society today."

Killian wished he had never started this conversation or therapy session or whatever it was. Far from sorting themselves out, his thoughts were only becoming more jumbled.

"We consume the souls of the dead or pull them out of the living by force if someone tries to help. How is that honorable?"

"Because despite your diverse backgrounds every one of you, every member of Sven's flock and mine, are in your situation for the same reason."

A strand from the tangled web of Killian's thoughts broke free and he clutched at it.

"We all sacrificed ourselves to save someone else."

"Exactly. And you did that without fully understanding what the consequences would be. Because you didn't care, as long as it meant the person you loved was safe."

"I guess I should give Sven some credit for showing honor of his own," Killian said begrudgingly. "He gave me a chance to back out."

"And why didn't you?"

"Because if I had, Sarah would have died. How could I live with that? Even if no one blamed me for her death, I would blame myself. *I'd* know the truth."

The web inside his mind was starting to unravel a little more.

"In other words," said Mir, "you made a difficult decision and followed through with it despite the pain it caused you, and despite being given a chance to back out. That is the very definition of honor. And you have shown your honor once again by deciding to join forces with myself and Edmund against Sven. Although you do not yet fully understand, your courage and sacrifice will help protect the ones you love."

"But I don't love the flock I'm betraying."

"Did I say they were the ones you would be protecting?"

"That's not what I meant. I meant—" Killian paused, trying to figure out the best way to phrase it. "If I don't even love them, then why is it this hard to turn against them?"

"Perhaps you feel the same connection with the rest of them that Sven does. Whether or not you love them—or even like them—is irrelevant; the mutual bond of respect is what binds you together."

It dawned on Killian slowly that what Mir was saying had merit. No matter what they were now, or what they did, all of Killian's flock mates had once been good people. People who cared enough to give up their own lives for someone they loved. And it was the same with him.

They flew on in silence for a while longer before Killian spoke again.

"Sven is eventually going to find out that Edmund and I are no longer on his side."

"That's why I'm teaching you to guard your mind."

"But even if we do nothing to advertise it beforehand, we'll have to show our true colors at some point by acting against him."

"This is true," Mir said slowly.

"You've known Sven for a lot longer than I have. Would he be likely to take out his anger on the whole flock, even if they had nothing to do with it?"

There was a thoughtful pause. "If you're asking if he would just outright kill them, the answer is no. A war is coming, and however high his confidence grows, he knows he cannot fight it alone. The members of his flock are the soldiers in his army. On the other side of the same coin, he would want to be absolutely certain that his soldiers remain loyal to him and him alone. I believe he would ask each of them to make the same choice that you and Edmund have already made."

"And if they choose to walk away from him?"

"Then I think they would have cause to regret that decision."

"So I'm putting them in danger as well by doing this."

"Yes," Mir answered. His bluntness surprised Killian, but it was still somehow refreshing after all the secrets that Sven kept. "I know that does not make you feel any more comfortable about your choice, but the fact that you bring it up at all shows that you have far more honor than Sven ever had or ever will have."

"I didn't even think about them when I made my decision," said Killian. It pained him to admit that, but he thought it would be best to come clean. "I was only thinking about the pain it would cause me if Sven did something to Sarah. Doesn't that make me more selfish than honorable?"

"It makes you *human*. And as I said, the fact that you thought of them at all shows a great deal about who you really are. Sven has always labored under the impression that you will become stronger if you give up human emotions like love and empathy. I believe the opposite. It was a big factor in what drove us apart."

"So pain and self-doubt are good?"

"In this case, yes. Seeing things through a lens that is still at least mostly human forces you to examine your own intentions. And while that process may not be pleasant, you come away with a much clearer picture of who you really are."

Killian did not reply. He understood Mir's point, but he wasn't sure he liked what he saw when he looked at himself.

When they reached their destination at last, Mir insisted that Killian have a few hours of rest to recover his strength before the training began. Killian agreed without argument, and when he slept he found himself once more dreaming about a great tree—the place that held all the answers for him. It was calling him, tugging at him with an ever-increasing urgency. He flew toward it all night, but it never seemed to get any closer. He woke up feeling vaguely disappointed that nothing else had happened. Then his feelings were overwhelmed by shock that was not his own, and he turned to see Mir scrutinizing him closely.

"What?" Killian asked, troubled by the other bird's demeanor.

"That tree you were dreaming of. Have you seen it before?"

"Twice, yes. But they're just dreams."

"That is a human's way of thinking," Mir told him scornfully. "Dreams carry much more importance for higher creatures like us. Now, explain to me what happened in this dream. I did not see all of it."

"I feel... called to this tree. Like I'll find understanding if I get there—only I always wake up before I reach my destination. What kind of meaning am I supposed to take from that?"

"That you are still on your journey. And if you stay on your current course, you are apt to discover the truths you are meant to find."

Killian got two distinct impressions. The first was that Mir was lying, or at least leaving out some pertinent information. The other was that this was not the time to discuss it, so he pretended to have noticed nothing.

"And what *is* the next step in my journey?" he asked Mir.

"The next step is your first lesson. Close your eyes."

Killian did so. Then Mir's voice came again. "Now keep them closed and find me."

Killian reached out with his mind, but his map didn't work out here, this far from Sven's borders. The location Mir had chosen meant that the teacher was stronger and the student was weaker. Then again, maybe that was the point. If he was strong enough to learn out here, he would be even stronger when he was back at full power.

"You're right," came Mir's voice from somewhere. "That is precisely the point. Now where am I?"

"I don't know. My telepathy—"

"Your telepathy works just fine. You just have to put in a bit more effort than you're used to."

So Killian took a deep breath and focused on Mir's voice. It was harder now that Mir wasn't actually speaking, but it was still something to latch onto. And this time he did feel something, behind a cluster of rocks to his left. The contact only lasted for a moment, yet it was there.

"You're behind the rocks."

"Open your eyes."

Killian obeyed and was shocked to see that he was now surrounded by owls of all shapes, sizes, and types. Where had they come from, and why had he not heard or otherwise sensed them? Owls were capable of flying quietly, but it was just a myth that they could move without making a sound. Wasn't it?

"Tell me what you see," came Mir's voice once again. And once again Killian latched onto it, but now it was coming from a different place.

"Company," Killian answered, looking at the dozen or so birds that formed a silent circle around him.

"Close your eyes again and tell me how many birds are in the near vicinity."

Killian's first instinct was to rely on memory, but he didn't think Mir was testing that. So he closed his eyes, listened to his too-rapid heartbeat for a few seconds, then began to listen for other things. He was surprised that the only other mind he felt was Mir's—and that wasn't really even a presence. It was just a wall so strong it was like a black hole, only discernible because it was even darker than the blackness that surrounded it.

"Amusing poetry," said Mir, in a tone that suggested he was anything but amused. "Now answer the question."

"There's just the two of us. And you've moved. You're not behind the rocks anymore."

"Then where am I?"

Killian reached out again but this time he could sense nothing at all, not even the barrier he'd felt before.

"I don't know," he answered Mir.

"Open your eyes."

Killian did, and barely managed not to topple over as he stumbled backward in shock. Mir was only a few inches in front of him, and there were no other birds to be seen.

"Did you just make me hallucinate?" Killian asked.

"Yes. You must to learn to recognize when your senses are being manipulated."

"Is someone manipulating my senses something that happens often?" He felt Mir's disapproval and hastily added, "I didn't mean that facetiously, I'm honestly curious."

"No, it does not happen often, but you must be prepared for any possibility. The Sven I once knew would never go so far, but he has changed so much over the years." He bowed his head for a moment, lost in some distant memory. Then he went on, "This lesson was meant to teach you not to rely on your physical senses too much. As long as you are focusing on them, you are holding yourself back from your full potential."

"I don't understand."

"Yet. You don't understand *yet*. But you will. Get a good night's sleep; you will need it for tomorrow."

Then he flew off, leaving Killian to watch him until he was out of sight. With so much to turn over in his mind he expected it would be a while until sleep came again for him. But exhaustion from the long flight won out, and he dropped off almost immediately into a dreamless sleep.

CHAPTER 14

Killian was alone when he awoke the next morning. He began foraging for food among the roots of the trees, and then suddenly wondered if he was really alone or if this was another test. He looked up from the ground and shook his feathers, then reached out with his mind, trying to find anything that felt like an intelligent life form. He was dismayed at how difficult it was—he kept instinctively trying to look at his mental map, forgetting it wasn't there. He didn't like the sensation of groping blindly in the dark, and his gut told him it could also be dangerous. He could stumble into a trap someone had laid for him—someone who was just waiting to try and mess with his mind.

Killian had closed his eyes while he was searching for Mir. Now he opened them and a powerful jolt of fear went through him. The darkness remained. He had been stricken blind! But how? Then logic reasserted itself and he realized he had been right in thinking Mir was teaching him another lesson. His eyesight returned all at once, and he blinked at the sudden light.

"Good," said a voice. Killian craned his neck upward, but the leaves were hiding Mir from view. "Why don't you come join me? If you can find me."

Killian kept his eyes open this time, but he didn't focus on what he was seeing. Most of his energy was devoted to finding that voice, and the power that gave it life. He turned slowly on the spot, looking around and feeling with his mind, and stopped when there was a reflection. At first he thought it was just the early-morning sunshine flashing off of something metallic; it was a moment before he realized he wasn't seeing that reflection with his physical eyes. He took off and flew toward it, confident. Sure enough, Mir was there inside a hollow tree that was cool and shaded.

"You've done well. Now tell me what you did wrong when we tried this last night."

At those words Killian flashed back to his first day of training as a seeker, up on Masonic Point with Charles. The answer he gave now was the same one he had given then.

"I was focused on the wrong thing. Last night I was trying to zero in on your voice, which was difficult because of the wall you'd built to block me out. But today I focused on *you*, not just your voice."

"You mean, 'the power that gave it life'?" Mir asked. His tone suggested that had he been human he would have been grinning and arching one eyebrow. "That's a direct quote from your own brain, by the way."

"Sounds kind of stupid now that I'm hearing someone else say it."

"Never mind how it sounds. What matters is that it was the right thing to do." He paused and then continued, "That power behind my voice—the same power is inside you as well. It's inside all living things to a certain degree, but it's stronger in the odedaud. Can you guess why that might be?"

"Because we absorb other people's light as well. When their souls pass through our circle."

"Exactly. That is what gives us life and strength, but it also makes each one of us unique. I might be able to hide my voice from you, even remove your ability to see or hear me, but I can no more hide that light than I can silence my heartbeat or stop my breathing."

"So that's what I have to focus on."

"Exactly."

"But how can I tell you apart from someone else? I can learn to find that 'reflection,' if that's the right word for it —like I did with you just now—but if everyone has one then how do I know whose reflection I'm seeing?"

"A wise question. But before you learn to go on the offensive and seek someone else out, you must first learn to stop yourself from being attacked and manipulated. So, I will now play with your mind and you will try to stop me."

Before Killian could mentally brace himself, he found he was unable to hear. This made him feel incredibly off-balance and very aware that he was a long way from the ground. So he focused on the part of his mind that controlled his ears, trying to push back against the force that was attacking it. Amazingly it seemed to work—he could hear again. Then Mir took away his vision, so Killian refocused his attention on regaining his sense of sight. But as soon as he succeeded and was able to see and hear, he felt himself falling. His flung his wings out and flapped them frantically, but he couldn't seem to rise.

"Look down," Mir told him. Killian did so and realized he was actually still standing on his branch, which explained why he wasn't gaining altitude. Even seeing the evidence with his own eyes, it took him a minute to realize what was happening. Instead of going after his sight or hearing, Mir had taken away his sense of touch, so he couldn't feel the branch that was supporting him. He found the point of attack in his mind and pushed back hard.

Mir went on blocking his senses in an endless circle until Killian was sure they had been going for hours. But when they paused for a break, the sun had barely moved at all; they must have only been at it for ten minutes. Killian felt weak and nauseous. He hoped he wasn't about to see his breakfast again.

Mir gave him a few minutes to collect himself, and then asked, "Do you know what you did wrong?"

"I countered every attack you threw at me," Killian replied, trying to keep the defensiveness in his tone to a bare minimum.

"Yes, you did. After I attacked you. Tell me, does it do any good to defend yourself from a knife that's already sticking out of your chest?"

"No."

"No," Mir repeated. "It does not. So, you take precautions to stop the knife in the first place: using a shield, dodging out of the way, that sort of thing. This is the comprehensive armor you must learn to construct around yourself. Since you don't know where I will attack from next, defend all fronts at once. Let's try again."

So the attacks resumed and continued for another ten minutes. Killian did marginally better this time—there were periods where he retained control over all his senses —but the effort left him feeling exhausted. It was going to be a very long day if he kept going at his current pace.

"You think the effort is only going to last for a day?" Mir asked, eavesdropping on Killian's inner musings. "This defense must be an absolute constant if you are to serve in Sven's inner circle while your true intentions remain hidden from him."

"But you're not teaching me how to guard my thoughts. You're just showing me how to defend against my physical senses being attacked."

"For now, yes. You cannot practice defending your inner thoughts without first mastering this skill."

Killian tried to build up a wall around himself as Natalie had taught him, partly because he wanted Mir out and partly because he wanted to see if he could do it with his telepathy so much weaker than it usually was. He failed on both accounts.

"Edmund has spoken highly of Natalie and her defensive skills. I sense there is some tension between you two."

"I wasn't even thinking about that until you brought it up."

"That goes to show the importance of what I'm trying to teach you. The subject of Natalie is clearly distracting to you. If I wanted to poke around undetected in other corners of your mind, I could manipulate you into thinking about her."

"Does Sven have that power as well?"

"Yes."

"And he could use it against Sarah if he was so inclined? To try and force her to give up on me?"

"Yes, I'm afraid so."

"And she would be defenseless if he tried to pull these kinds of tricks on her."

"Yes," Mir said again. "Just as you are defenseless at the moment."

"Then let's go. I'm ready to try again."

By around noon that day, Killian was able to throw off Mir's extrasensory attacks completely.

"Excellent work," said Mir as they ate a small lunch together. "We're running ahead of the schedule I'd planned out for us."

"I have a good teacher," said Killian, finishing his last bite. "So what's next?"

"As I'm sure you already know, there are different levels to a person's mind. On the top are the physical sensations. Underneath lie the person's memories, the internal dialogue they have with themselves, and the subconscious thoughts and feelings they may not even be aware of. It is this second level you must learn to guard at all costs. It involves the same basic technique you've been using, but you'll have to venture deeper into your own mind to make it work. Are you ready for your first attempt?"

"Yes," said Killian.

And then the world around him vanished and all he

could see was Sarah. He was on one knee in front of her. There was a beaming smile on her face and happy tears in her eyes. Then his point of view shifted downward and he was looking at his own hand holding hers, putting a diamond ring onto her finger. Before he could relish the memory for very long it had slipped away and he was once again surrounded by the deserted forests of northeastern Idaho.

"Not to ruin your happiness, but you were supposed to try and stop me from doing that."

"I remember the night I proposed to her, but I didn't know I remembered every detail like that."

"The details are buried deep in your subconscious. I simply brought them to the surface and overwhelmed your physical senses along the way. In other words, I distracted you. That allowed me to discover that your first pet was a border collie named Chloe. Your mother adopted her from a shelter shortly after your father passed."

"I couldn't even feel you poking around in there," said Killian. "I haven't thought about Chloe in years."

"So now you have that emotional pain to distract you as well. You've given me yet another weapon to add to my arsenal."

Killian tried to think of a wall again, but found himself thinking about a poker game instead. He was holding five cards and there were a handful of plastic chips in the center of the green felt tabletop in front of him. The cards formed a royal flush, but he couldn't let the other players know that.

"Interesting," Mir said quietly, recalling him to the present.

"What is?"

"Perhaps Natalie was teaching you in the wrong way. The wall couldn't keep me out when you tried it before, but when you thought about that poker game just now, I couldn't sense the sadness you were feeling about your first dog or your annoyance at me for bringing it to the surface in the first place."

"Really?"

"You were only able to keep me out for a few seconds but yes, really. Let's try again, shall we?"

This time Killian found himself remembering his very first day at school, when he had cried and begged his mother not to leave him. The memory was still powerful enough to overwhelm his physical senses, but this time he was *aware* that it was affecting him that way. And the details of this memory were not quite as sharp as they had been with the first one. He thought of a royal flush and caught a brief glimpse of a raven sitting on his mother's left shoulder as she assured him everything would be alright.

Then his mother was gone and only the raven remained.

"Better. It was harder to me to attack you, and easier for you to push me out, even if you couldn't stop me completely. But I was still able to look through some of your other thoughts and feelings while you were otherwise engaged."

"And what did you find?" Killian asked, suddenly apprehensive.

"That you still miss your father, even though you no longer believe you were responsible for his death."

That cut far deeper than Killian's memories of Chloe.

163

He had thought those feelings about his father were gone forever, buried deep within his subconscious. Clearly not, if Mir had been able to discover that as a very young boy Killian had wished that his father would finally be able to find some peace. When his father died the next day, Killian had panicked, thinking he'd wished too hard. He had never spoken to anyone about those feelings, and had recognized them as nonsense when he got older. But if they were still in his head, then what else was down there?

"*Everything* is down there," Mir answered his unasked question. "Everything is stored indefinitely, but most people don't know how to access it. Your abilities as an odedaud give you more of a chance than humans; you could examine every word you've ever spoken, if you so desired."

"I don't desire."

"Nor would I recommend it. But you need to understand that all of these things are weapons that could be used against you if they fall into the wrong hands. I am bringing up your past demons to teach you, not to be cruel."

"I know," said Killian. "But that doesn't stop it from hurting. Still, I know Sven could do a lot worse."

"That he could. He and I are just about equal in strength, but his intent is much more malicious than mine. That makes a great deal of difference."

"Let's try again, then."

With the third attempt, Killian found himself thinking of his wedding day, but this time he could see something else too. Sarah was standing there in her white dress, yet there was something worse right behind her. Somewhat reluctantly he put the wedding out of his mind and focused on whatever was floating behind the happy memory. Now instead of seeing Sarah in a wedding gown he saw her lying unconscious on the floor; he was leaning toward her to attempt resuscitation, heedless of the voices that warned him against it.

No! he thought. *It's not real. It's just another lesson.*

That realization was enough to make him regain his physical senses; he looked around, seeing not Sarah but Mir, and a deserted pine forest.

"You pushed me out," Mir said approvingly.

"So that wasn't just you letting up and giving me my eyesight back?"

"Not at all. That was very impressive for just your third try."

"Thank you. But it helps because I know you're attacking me. I know what I'm seeing isn't real."

"True," Mir replied, and his voice was thoughtful. Then he asked, "How *did* you know it wasn't real? Because you remembered your present situation, or because you could just feel something off?"

"A combination of both, I think. I could see Sarah on our wedding day, but I could also see her on the floor in our living room, the night Sven turned me. Was that the other memory you were examining?"

"Yes."

"Well I saw that, and then I remembered that none of what I was seeing was real."

"I see. In a way, you were successful. But it goes back to your first mistakes this morning. You launched a counterstrike instead of defending yourself from being attacked in the first place."

"I waited until the knife was sticking out of my chest," Killian said, recalling Mir's words from earlier.

"Exactly. It may help you to concentrate on the 'reflection' that I give off, the same thing that let you find me this morning. Focus on locating that within your own head, and you'll figure out where I'm about to attack. Are you ready?"

Killian gave his assent and immediately started searching for Mir's light. He was surprised at the ease with which he found it. And he still had full control of his physical senses, even though he wasn't currently focused on the world around him. He was entirely inside his own mind, following Mir's light around and trying not to be distracted by the snatches of his own memories he was catching as they went.

I'm channel surfing inside my own head, he thought with a flash of amusement.

Then he remembered that just following Mir around wasn't going to do any good. He darted off ahead of the light and blocked its way. The reflection that was actually his mentor tried to swerve around him, but Killian blocked it again, not giving an inch. This went on for about five minutes before the light winked out. He looked through his physical eyes again and saw Mir's bright, intelligent stare.

"Now *that* was certainly progress," he said, and Killian basked in the fierce pride rolling off of Mir like a gentle wave.

CHAPTER 15

By early afternoon, Killian could not only identify when Mir was inside his head, he could build up a protective barrier that was strong but also subtle—so subtle as to almost be invisible. Mir had been right that Natalie wasn't teaching him in quite the right way. Killian thought of his barrier not as a wall built to keep out enemies but as a poker face.

"I have one more thing to teach you before we depart for your own territory. By now you know when someone is intruding on your thoughts, and you know how to stop those intrusions from happening. You've also shown your ability to push back and counter with attacks of your own. But if someone did manage to slip past your defenses, it is useful to know who is digging around in your mind.

"This lesson is more difficult to teach because I'm the only one here; if you feel someone looking at your thoughts, it is me. But each bird's life force, or reflection, is unique, just as every human being's personality is different. I sense you are already familiar with that concept?"

"Yes," Killian replied. "It's how I learned to build my mental map."

"Show me."

Killian brought up a blank map in his mind and let down his defensive barrier enough to let Mir see. Then, while Mir watched, he made two dots appear on it.

"I sort of zoomed in on each of the dots," said Killian, demonstrating as he spoke. "And then I listened to their thoughts until I figured out who it was. Then a little label appeared above the dot, and from there I just learned to keep it in the back of my mind at all times."

"The back of your mind is becoming quite a busy place, with you having to maintain your constant defense," Mir commented. "And you leave yourself open to detection if you have to go nosing around in someone else's thoughts to find out who they are."

"What if I concentrate on having the wall built up around my light while I'm doing it?" Killian suggested. "Hold a shield in one hand and a sword in the other."

"An apt metaphor, and a sound strategy as well. You really are a good student, Killian. I can see why Edmund singled you out to be part of our mission."

Again, Killian got the nagging feeling that Mir wasn't telling the whole truth. It was something about the way he paused ever so slightly before saying Edmund's name. But again, he also got the feeling that now was not the time to discuss it.

"Why don't you try with me now?" Mir said. "I want to see if I can feel you in there."

Killian dove in. Mir kept his thoughts well guarded,

and Killian couldn't find a way in, but he was at least able to see what he was doing while still keeping himself cloaked.

"Again," Mir said after a little while. "You're quiet, but I can still feel you, like a mosquito buzzing in my ear."

So, he tried again. This time he thought he saw a glimpse of the same tree he had dreamed about, before Mir forcefully pushed him out.

"You were focused more on your sword than your shield and that gave you away," said Mir. "Before that you were doing well. I could feel you a little bit, but that might just be because I knew I should be looking for something." He paused, then looked up at the sky and said, "I'm proud of how far you've come in such a short time, but I think that's all the training we have time for. We should start heading back to your own territory, so you can give Sven your answer. Although I would like to try one more experiment before you're back within his telepathic range."

"What kind of experiment?"

"The kind I won't tell you about, just to ensure I get an honest result."

The flight back was uneventful, with Killian enjoying the scenery below him while he tried to relax his mind as much as possible in order to conserve his energy. Mir called a halt to the journey when they were still some distance from Sven's border, coming down to land in the lightning-struck tree where Killian's journey had begun the day before. Edmund joined them after a few minutes.

"How did the training go?" he said by way of greeting. The question was addressed to Killian, but Mir was the one who answered.

"He is an extraordinarily gifted individual, and a very quick learner. Your instincts about him were correct. Could I have a word with you before I go, Edmund?"

"Of course," Edmund replied.

"Good. Killian, wait here for us."

Mir and Edmund spread their wings and flew toward the next hill, which was about a mile away. Killian watched them until they faded from sight. Was this something to do with the dream he'd had last night, the one Mir seemed so concerned about?

Killian felt more than heard a buzzing noise and shook his head to shoo away any insects. When the buzzing persisted, Killian realized it was coming from inside his own head. Someone was looking for information. Setting aside a small part of his mind to focus on protecting his innermost thoughts, he devoted the rest of his mental prowess toward finding the intruder. He sensed the entity's light quickly enough and stealthily gave chase. When he got close enough he reached out with his own light, breaking through the surface of the intruder's thoughts and landing in a memory of the city of London; a small boy was on the street corner selling newspapers.

Now who did he know who spoke with a British accent? Killian drew back, pushed Edmund out of his head entirely, and then said, "So you used to sell newspapers on the streets of London, did you, Edmund? Could I help you find something particular inside my head or were you just browsing?"

"He *is* good," Edmund said, clearly addressing Mir. Then he added, "We're heading back now, be there in a minute."

When they returned, Mir said, "It has been a pleasure

teaching you and I'm sure we will see each other again soon. This is where I leave you, but I will offer one final piece of advice before I go: don't go poking around in Sven's thoughts the way you did with Edmund's. For that matter, don't do it with any stranger trespassing inside your mind. Learn to identify people by their light alone, so you don't fall into a trap."

"Not to mention if Sven found you inside his head, he would not be pleased," Edmund added. "And the odds are good that he would find you."

With a final word of farewell, Mir left them.

"So what now?" Killian asked after they had watched the raven disappear from view.

"Sven wants to meet you at sundown at the top of Crater Ridge. He sent me to tell you. But you've still got half an hour, and he might think it's suspicious if you arrive early. Do what you want, then meet us there."

"Right. Thanks, Edmund."

They flew off in separate directions, Killian letting his wings pick their own path. When the sun began to go down in earnest, he headed toward the appointed meeting place. This was not an interview he wanted to be late for. When he arrived he focused entirely on the pain his encounter with Sarah and John had caused him. He kept up that subtle wall inside his head the way Mir had taught him, but let his pain seep out through the cracks; it would give Sven something to latch onto, and that would hopefully keep him from asking too many questions.

Killian landed on the rocky outcropping on top of the ridge and looked out at the darkening sky. He could just make out the scenic lookout point where he had proposed to Sarah. It seemed fitting that since his journey had started here, it was where the next step should originate.

"And have you decided what that step will be?" came Sven's voice.

Killian had sensed Sven and Edmund's presence in his head, but he feigned surprise.

"Yes," he said, turning around. "I want to accept the offer you extended."

"Why?" the two members of the inner circle asked in unison.

"Because the past few days have given me time to reflect on my humanity—what's left of it, anyway. And I've come to realize you were right when you said that human emotions can be a burden."

"Very well," Sven replied, and asked no more questions. Killian didn't feel anyone poking around in his mind either. "You will rejoin the flock tonight, but you will not speak to anyone. In the morning, when everyone leaves to take their accustomed places, you will remain with us. We will explain more about your duties tomorrow, in private. Is that understood?"

"Yes."

Killian took flight with Sven and Edmund, heading to rejoin his flock—his family—and take his new place within it.

CHAPTER 16

That first night back was the worst by far. The fact that the other two seekers ignored him was not out of the ordinary, although Charles had spared him a curious glance before going back to sharpening his talons against a rock. Then Natalie came up to him as he was settling down for the night. Before he blocked her out, he sent off a wave of apology, hoping she would understand that the silent treatment he was giving her was nothing personal. Her head drooped sadly, but she left him alone.

Killian could feel someone, probably Edmund, keeping a close eye on him, so he resisted the strong urge to build up a wall around himself and Natalie and talk to her anyway. But that would only make the separation harder, and it would be best to stay on Sven's good side for as long as possible given what he would eventually have to do. He cut that line of thought off hard before it could escape his defensive barrier and focused instead on remembering the rules of poker. The repetitive cycle of thought simultaneously calmed him and acted as a shield. It came as no surprise to him that, when he finally slept, he dreamed of playing cards with Gavin and Rick.

The next morning, Sven called them all to himself as usual.

"You know your places. Charles, Randall, your hunting grounds have been restored to what they were before Killian joined your ranks. Fly, and may we meet safely once more."

They left, Natalie looking straight ahead but reaching back with her mind, curious and pained. With Sven watching him, Killian didn't dare try to respond in any way, even though it hurt him to ignore her. She deserved better than this; he could only hope that one day he would get the chance to explain himself.

"You have much to learn if you are to help us," Sven told him. "As I told you earlier, one of the conditions of this position is that you belong to us completely. This is a position that requires your full powers of concentration at all times. You cannot afford to be distracted by anything—or anyone—else. That includes any human friends you may still have."

"I understand," Killian said, and tried to hide the sorrow in his heart.

"Edmund will teach you how to guard your thoughts from the rest of the flock, but I would warn you strongly against trying to shut us out as well. There will be... unpleasant consequences if you do."

Again, Killian indicated his understanding.

"You will train with Edmund today. I have business elsewhere, so I leave you in his capable care."

Sven left without another word and Killian felt Edmund's wall go up around them.

"Obviously I don't need to teach you how to guard your thoughts."

"No, you don't."

"Did Mir teach you how to falsify emotions as well?"

"What do you mean?"

"Sven wasn't the only one who could feel your thoughts last night. The pain, anger, and fear were very convincing. And they were all to be expected of course, given your position. I just find them a bit interesting, given how confident you seemed in your decision to go against Sven and bring him down."

Killian said nothing.

"The thoughts and emotions you were projecting last night," Edmund prompted him, "the ones you're projecting right now—are those real, or just part of the act?"

"Real. But none of it has to do with my decision."

"Mir was right. You *are* good. Do you even realize how hard you're fighting to hide your thoughts from me? But that just makes me curious about what you don't want me to find."

"Sorry, does this actually matter?"

"It might. Because maybe I can help."

"I really don't think you can," Killian said. Then he relented, knowing Edmund would not let the matter drop until he got an answer. "Sven thinks he can manipulate Sarah's thoughts as a means of keeping me with him, right?"

"Right."

175

"If he waits a little while longer, he might not need to manipulate her at all."

Edmund was quiet for a few seconds. Then he said, "She's losing her faith in you."

"Yes."

"Would you be surprised if I said I knew what you were going through?"

"Yes. I would be," said Killian. Then he said, "You... don't have to talk about it if you don't want to."

"But you're curious." He laughed when he felt Killian's wall inch up a little higher. "Don't worry, you didn't let that out through the cracks in your defense. I just know how people think."

"I'm not a person anymore."

It was strange, saying it so baldly like that.

"Maybe not, but you still retain your personality—your 'reflection' as I believe Mir calls it. My wife waited a long time for me. She might have waited even longer, if we had been living in today's time. But medical knowledge was not nearly so advanced in the early 1900s."

"You've been alive for almost a century?"

"Closer to a century and a half. I was forty-two when I changed, in 1919."

"I'm sorry."

"Why? Because I'm an old man who can never die of old age? Or because this may one day be your fate as well?"

"Sorry for bringing up the past. It's not like either of us can go back and change anything. The deal we made was permanent."

"I wouldn't change it even if I could," Edmund said.

"As much pain as I caused my Catherine, and as much as I know it hurt her to finally let me go, she was able to make a good life for herself. She was happy. And to me that makes the sacrifice worth it."

"Agreed," Killian said, and was surprised to find how sincerely he meant it. But wasn't that the reason he had said yes to Sven's offer in the first place? So that Sarah would have a chance to be happy? It seemed he had forgotten about that at some point.

"Are you done dwelling on the past?" Edmund asked, after giving him some space.

"Yes."

"Good. Then let's talk about the future, and specifically about what's next for you." He dropped the protective wall around them, and Killian understood it was a precaution in case Sven decided to listen in and observe their training session.

"As Sven explained, our plan is to have you determine from afar whether or not a potential victim is going to make it," Edmund went on. "To do that, you must learn to cast your telepathic net further afield than you're currently used to. You proved in your first day of training as a seeker that you could read people from a distance, but it exhausted you, and exhaustion isn't an option if the flock does end up having to gather."

"Because I might have to help you take someone's soul from their body."

"One thing at a time. I was more thinking along the lines that we might lose the soul altogether if the person dies before we all get there and start circling. If you're too tired to keep up, in other words. Let's see how well you do on your own before I give you any instruction. That way we'll have a baseline to start from. Stay here."

Edmund flew a short distance away from him, about ten yards.

"I'm thinking of a color," he told Killian. "On the count of three, you will tell me what that color is. Ready? One, two, three."

Killian focused in and answered easily, "Red."

"Good." Edmund increased the distance to twenty yards. "One, two, three."

"Green," Killian answered. The thought from Edmund's mind had been a little quieter, but still something he could pick up on without too much difficulty.

"Right," said Edmund. He increased the distance again —now he was almost thirty yards away. "One, two, three."

"Purple," said Killian, noticing that this time he had to strain a little bit to hear.

"Good." Now Edmund flew all the way to the top of a tree just on the edge of Killian's vision; he was little more than a shadow in the uppermost branches. "One, two, three."

"Umm... Yellow."

Edmund flew back down to where Killian stood. "Why did you hesitate that last time?"

"It was harder for me to hear you."

"Why?"

"Because of the distance, I guess."

"You will be reading people from a far greater distance than that. And you'll be looking for something much deeper and more complex than a color they're thinking of. Close your eyes."

Killian did as he was told, half expecting Edmund to start attacking his senses.

"Now what color am I thinking of?"

"Blue?"

"You're right, but that sounded like a guess to me. Open your eyes again."

Killian did so and was surprised to find that Edmund was still standing right next to him.

"Were you blocking me?"

"No," Edmund answered. "You were relying too much on your physical senses. You were so focused on not being able to see me that you forgot to listen to what was going on inside my head. And in the previous exercises you assumed that because I was farther away, it would be harder to hear me. But you don't need to listen with your physical ears."

Again, Killian felt Edmund's protective barrier surround them both. "Remember what Mir taught you."

"Right."

"Now try again," said Edmund, dropping the wall. "But this time keep your focus on my thoughts, not on whether or not you can see me. You already have a connection with me, so that should make it easier."

"I won't have a connection with the people I'm tracking," Killian pointed out.

"No, but as I said, we are focusing on one thing at a time. And besides, you wouldn't be tracking our victims, necessarily. It is possible to take over the senses of another member of the flock."

"I know," Killian said without thinking—a quickly stifled flash of anger from Edmund reminded him that he wasn't supposed to know that.

"Natalie taught me," he added, trying to cover his mistake. "When I was first paired up with her she sort of... guided me. She kept my mind focused on what she was seeing."

"That's an effective method of teaching. I didn't realize she even knew how to do that." The pride in Edmund's voice was sarcastic on the surface, although Killian thought it might be real underneath. "You have a lot to learn before we get to that point, though. Let's begin."

And that was the pattern that developed for Killian: training day in and day out while learning about the offensive side of telepathy, which was all Sven seemed to care about. After two weeks, Sven and Edmund gave him his first assignment: judging the veracity of a call from afar. Charles was the one who put out the signal, so Killian was already confident it would be a valid claim, but he reminded himself that he should not let that color his opinion. From his perch on top of a rock in the middle of a lake, Killian closed his eyes and felt his way toward Charles. Edmund had taught him how to use the voices of the others like a fishing line. He used that now to reel himself in toward Charles' location. Then he took over the other bird's eyes so he could look down at the victim. It was a child this time, a little girl, and Killian felt a pang go through him at that. Then he realized that had probably influenced Charles' decision to sound the alarm—he was assuming that someone would interfere and try to help.

Killian got inside the little girl's mind, and the dark streak he found there was curiously strong. He thought she must have some underlying or chronic condition. He dug around a little more; this was the first one that Sven and Edmund were trusting him on, so he wanted to be sure. He could feel pain in the girl's chest, even though she was far too young to be feeling anything of the sort. That more than anything convinced him that the child was going to die, with or without someone's interference.

Killian retreated back into his own head, and opened his eyes. The calm, gray waters surrounding him were a stark contrast to what he'd just experienced.

"We should go," said Killian, addressing Sven. "She's not going to make it."

As Sven, Edmund, and Killian started toward the site of the event, Sven said, "Remember what you have been taught again and again: your humanity burdens you. Take comfort from the fact that her death will not be in vain; it will feed us and make us strong."

"I know."

"You will help us kill her if it comes to that."

Sven's voice was stern, and Killian knew his protests would do no good. Since he had joined the inner circle, they had only encountered natural deaths; the person had died as a result of their injuries or illness, not because someone else stretched out a hand to offer assistance. To actually help Sven and Edmund take the life would be a much harder pill to swallow.

"I don't know how it's done," said Killian, hiding his distaste but not bothering to hold back his overall anxiety.

"Sven and I will be doing the majority of the work," Edmund told him. "You'll just be providing a little extra muscle to make things easier."

Not sure if he should be comforted by that or not, Killian was silent for the rest of the flight. They had barely started their circle when a woman, presumably the girl's mother, rushed out of the house and ran to the swing set where the girl had been playing. Killian made sure to stay out of the woman's head—he didn't want to feel her pain and fear in addition to his own. The woman reached out to hold the child, unaware of the consequences that would bring.

"It is time," Sven announced. Then, privately, he added to Killian, "Join us in the center of the circle."

Killian did as he was told and felt his mind be taken over; he was drawn into the child's head, with Sven and Edmund by his side.

Killian asked Edmund, "What exactly are you expecting me to do?"

"Just focus on the death streak for now. I'll guide you more once we're down there."

Killian obeyed, trying to sense only the darkness at the bottom of the little girl's mind and not her fading memories, the deepening tightness and pressure in her chest, or her mother's sadness and fear. They were right above that dark abyss now, and there seemed to be some kind of force field around it. Was that the mother's love trying to protect her child from death? Or was that too romantic a notion to actually be true?

"Focus, Killian!" Edmund snapped at him.

"Don't pull away, no matter how frightened you get," Sven added. "Not only will it make things much harder for us, it will also be a less peaceful demise for the little one."

Killian wasn't sure if the regret he heard in Sven's tone was real or imagined, but he took courage from it all the same. He didn't care much about the peace and comfort of his fellow odedaud, but he wanted to make things as easy as possible for the child, especially since she was so young. All of this rushed through Killian's head in the space of about two seconds, and in those two seconds he was drawn inexorably on toward the dark streak and the shield around it. He braced himself for impact as they got closer to the guarding light, but he needn't have worried. They sank through easily, as though the shield were no more substantial than the surface of a soap bubble.

Inside the darkness now, Killian sensed vague shapes and wisps of shadow moving all around them, although he did not dare to examine them more closely. In an effort to keep himself balanced and grounded he focused on the connection that he had with Sven and Edmund. He needed that balance now, because he was being buffeted back and forth. Those shapes and shadows had sensed the intruders and were not happy about it. Undeterred, Sven and Edmund dove still deeper into the abyss, with Killian following along behind. They must be nearing the bottom of this dark sea by now, but there was an immense pressure all around them, as if the darkness had a physical weight—it was getting harder and harder to withstand. Edmund sent out a streak of light from his mind. The shadows backed away and Killian enjoyed a temporary relief. But when the light faded, the shadows converged on them again.

"Killian, do the same thing I just did," said Edmund. Keeping in mind that his actions would ultimately help the child, Killian sent out his own streak of light. Even though it was not as strong as Edmund's, it got the job done, and they were granted a temporary reprieve. Killian thought he saw light ahead of them, but then it was swallowed up by shadows once more.

"Give us another blast, as big as you can manage it," Sven ordered. "Then you'll see what we're aiming for."

Killian used up most of his remaining energy on the second attack, but he still needed help from Edmund to drive away the shadows.

"Look down," Edmund said now.

Killian did, and saw something that reminded him of a tree stump, but it was made entirely of light—that was what he had glimpsed through the shadows. Tendrils of illumination spread from this main source, but they were thin and fading fast, shriveling up until there was nothing left. As Killian watched, Sven sent a bolt of light out from his mind and it severed the last root as easily as an axe felling a tree.

Without warning, Killian found himself rocketing backward into his own mind, now seeing things from a distance. The light of the overcast day was dazzling to him after the darkness inside the child's mind. Then he felt the now-familiar streak of pure energy pass through their circle and helped the rest of the group harvest the power the soul created, keeping his mind as blank as possible. It was only when they were all flying home that he allowed his restless thoughts to center on the fact that the light they'd just absorbed had been fighting hard to stay connected to its vessel. And he had helped to sever that connection. He felt sick to his stomach at the thought.

"You didn't destroy it," said Edmund privately, and for once Killian didn't care that his thoughts were being listened to without his permission. "It—and the vessel— would have suffered later on in life."

"But at least she would have *had* a life," Killian retorted.

He knew Edmund was only trying to help, but he resented the older bird all the same. Sensing that, Edmund left him alone with only his thoughts for company.

CHAPTER 17

Two months passed, and two more victims were taken because of a bystander's interference. The shock of diving into someone's essence was not as bad as it had been the first time, and although Killian doubted he would ever come to enjoy it, he thought maybe he could learn to live with it. But the horror he felt when the act was actually committed had not diminished in the slightest. He thought he understood now why Sven had advised him to give up his humanity: it would have made things easier, and maybe he wouldn't feel so much like a murderer, as they took the lives of people whose only crime was that someone cared enough to reach out and help. At the same time, Killian didn't want to let go of that human connection—that part of his mind that questioned the morality of his actions. Without it, he truly would be no better than a murderer.

Killian didn't know how Sven was able to stand being the one who actually severed the soul from the person's body. Maybe *that* was why their leader's voice was so distant and cold when he spoke, why he spent so much time alone. It was out of pure necessity. Having the ability to take a life at will was enough to drive anyone crazy, and quickly. Yet, Killian could not deny that the power was somehow intoxicating as well. He tried to push away the thought whenever it came to his mind, but he could not keep it away indefinitely. Maybe that was truly the last aspect of his humanity he was holding onto: the part that was so easily corrupted by power.

In spite of his doubts, Killian held fast to his decision, learning everything he could from Sven in case he ever had to use those tactics for himself. Then again, maybe that day would never come. Maybe Sven and Mir would just stay out of each other's way.

But this wishful thinking soon came to an end.

There came a night when Edmund flew back to their roosting spot after checking the perimeter, listening for anyone who knew or suspected more than they should. He was obviously distracted by something, and just as obviously trying not to let it show. This immediately got Killian's attention, but Edmund's wall was impenetrable when he tried to look.

"I wouldn't do that if I were you," he growled in Killian's head. Then, projecting not just to Killian anymore, he said, "Sven? A word in private?"

"Killian, you're in charge while we're away."

They flew off together, leaving Killian alone with the rest of the flock, who largely ignored him. But Natalie took advantage of Sven and Edmund's absence and came over to talk.

"What was that all about?" she asked, and Killian could feel that she was shielding them from the others.

"No idea," he answered her, adding his own wall to hers. "Something private that apparently doesn't concern me."

"I thought they shared everything with you now. You're part of their group, aren't you?"

"Hardly. I wish they'd never asked me to join."

"But they *did* ask you," Natalie said. "If you hate it so much, why would you say yes?"

"I'm doing what I have to do," he said quietly, keeping his true intentions locked deep inside.

"What could possibly justify—"

"It doesn't concern you," he interrupted, unaware of just how much he sounded like Sven in that moment. Then he shut himself off from her, pretending not to feel her anger and confusion at why he was treating her this way. But he was only trying to protect her; it would be dangerous if she knew what was going on.

Edmund came back, alone.

"Where's our fearless leader?" Natalie asked hotly, causing Randall and Charles to look over in surprise. Her temper had apparently translated into a kind of reckless courage.

"Taking care of things which only concern the fearless leader," Edmund answered. "There is no cause for alarm."

Natalie flew off in a huff without responding; apparently her courage only stretched so far.

"What's really going on?" Killian asked.

"Nothing," Edmund replied, but Killian knew he was lying. He also knew that trying to find the answer would not get him anywhere, so he let the matter drop, or at least pretended to. But he still kept an eye on Edmund, who was staring off into the distance to the south. He felt

Edmund's mind, his mental reflection, disappear for about thirty seconds—then it was back, and more closely guarded than ever.

Suddenly Charles looked up from the rock he'd been using to sharpen his talons and asked, "Did you feel that?"

"It feels like a summoning call," said Edmund. He sounded puzzled, but Killian thought the confusion was just an act.

"Is it Sven?" asked Randall.

"Well clearly it's not any of us," Edmund replied shortly. The call came again, and it was more urgent this time—urgent enough to make them all flinch.

"Sounds like we'd better go," Edmund said.

With little other choice, they all rose into the air and headed in the direction the call was coming from. Edmund set a fast pace, but Killian knew he could have gone faster if he'd wanted to—he was holding back for some reason. And Killian couldn't be sure, but it also seemed that Edmund was talking to somebody else long-distance while keeping everyone blocked out.

He's probably just telling Sven we're on our way, Killian tried to reassure himself, but he couldn't shake the nagging feeling that there was something more going on. Then, Edmund spoke to Killian privately.

"Get ready," he said. "If Sven felt strongly enough to have us fly at night, he must be pretty confident about the outcome."

After about twenty minutes, they reached their leader, who was riding on a current of air above a dark, two-lane road. At first Killian thought the road was empty, but then he reached out with his mental eyes and sensed one of the strongest death streaks he'd ever felt.

"About time you all showed up," Sven barked. "I was flying over the road when I witnessed a car accident, hit and run. It seemed like too good of an opportunity to pass up, so I called you all here. The man's lucky to still be alive, but he won't be for much longer. Now get to work; you know what to do."

So they began their slow circling, putting the count-down of one hour into motion. Thirty minutes passed and the man below them still clung to life, although by a bare thread to judge from the darkness growing inside him. But Killian tried his best to stay out of the victim's mind. Keeping his distance did make things easier; Sven had been right about that, if nothing else.

When forty-five minutes had gone by, Killian began to feel a cautious hope. Sven, by contrast, was undeniably frustrated. Just the fact that Killian could sense his feel-ings was evidence enough. What was so special about this particular victim that was making Sven forget to hide his thoughts?

Breaking his own self-enforced rule, Killian decided to look into the mind of the man they were circling. But the darkness overwhelmed everything about his identity. Killian had never seen that happen before. It was almost as if that darkness wasn't coming from the death streak, but from someone putting up a block. Were they trying to make the death streak appear stronger than it actually was? But why?

"Edmund, this doesn't make sense," Killian said quietly, careful to keep it hidden from Sven. "Something's not right here."

Before Edmund could reply, they saw a car pull over to the side of the road. A passerby stopping to help? That would give the flock the cosmic permission they needed to go in for the kill and end it, but Killian was no longer sure he wanted that to happen. Then the passerby's headlights illuminated the victim on the ground and even from this distance the whole flock recognized who it was. At least Killian now understood why Sven had been hiding the victim's identity.

"John!" Natalie cried, moving as if to break out of the circle.

"Stay where you are!" Sven said sharply. She didn't dare disobey, but Killian didn't blame her for wanting to fly down to John's side. He had half a mind to do it himself.

"Stop it, Killian," came Edmund's voice. He spoke deep in Killian's mind, hidden from all the others, including Sven. "Put your emotions aside for once and just listen. If we betray Sven now he'll block us out and then kill John anyway."

"We can't just sit back and let it happen!"

"Who said anything about doing that? Wait until we're inside, and then go on the attack against Sven. The time has come to show our true colors. Can you do that?"

"Y-yes," Killian stammered out.

"Then get ready."

Killian looked down at the ground again in time to see the driver of the car that had stopped to help leap out and run to John's side. He was stirring, but only a little. Then the Good Samaritan, whoever it was, reached out to check John's pulse.

"Now!" Sven cried, with savage triumph. He swooped

downward with his mind, pulling Killian and Edmund along for the ride. The descended quickly through the swirls of light and color that were John's memories, headed for the bottom of his mind.

"Stop, Sven!" Edmund cried suddenly, and Sven whirled around to face him. "John was once one of us; he has proven himself honorable."

Sven gave a shriek of mirthless laughter. "John sacrificed his honor when he betrayed me."

"I will not help you do this," said Edmund, his calm voice a stark contrast to Sven's. But underneath the facade, Killian could sense him tensing and flexing every mental and physical muscle, getting ready for what was coming.

"You knew what you would be asked to do when you joined my flock. You accepted those responsibilities. Do you defy them now? Do you defy *me*?"

"Yes," Edmund answered simply.

"And you, boy?" Sven asked Killian.

"I won't help you commit murder," Killian replied, using all of his emotion as fuel for his mental fire.

"Then stay out of my way," said Sven, and he dove alone into the darkness at the bottom of John's mind.

"Now what?" Killian demanded of Edmund.

"Now you harness your fear and hold Sven off for as long as you can. I'm going to turn John back into one of us."

"You can do that?"

"I watched Sven turn all the other members of this flock, including you. I've never tried to execute the process myself, but I don't see another option. Once John is an odedaud again he'll be able to help us."

"Good luck," said Killian. It seemed comically inadequate given the circumstances, but it was all he could think of to say.

"Likewise."

And then Edmund's light was gone from Killian's head as Killian himself dove into the depths of John's mind, following the dim speck of light that was Sven. When Killian was almost upon him, Sven stopped and then changed direction. Apparently he had sensed what Edmund was up to. Killian got in front of him, with wings of light outstretched to block the path forward. He pushed everything else out of his mind—what Edmund was doing now, his own terror, the way John's life hung in the balance—and focused only on the light that he himself was emanating. The rush of power and confidence it gave him was incredible.

"Get out of my way," Sven growled, veering left. But in his anger he neglected to block his intentions, so Killian knew he was only faking and blocked him again with ease.

"I gave you life!" Sven cried. "I gave you this power and taught you how to harness it. You dare use it against me?"

"Yes, I dare!" said Killian, still refusing to give an inch of ground despite Sven's best efforts. "*I* get to decide what I do with the gifts you gave me. That's where my power lies."

"Then you'll have to live with the consequences of your choices."

White-hot light shot out toward Killian and he flinched aside instinctively. Sven took full advantage and surged past. Furious with himself, Killian turned and pursued his prey. Sven was taking them higher, up toward

John's memories and physical senses. Amidst the snatches of memory and thought he was picking up, Killian also saw a warm light, growing brighter all the time. *So that's what Sven's heading for,* he thought.

Knowing he couldn't let Edmund down, Killian fired a bolt of light out ahead of himself, directly into Sven's path. It had the desired effect of making him change course, but now he was coming directly for Killian.

"You will not win against me, boy," said Sven, his voice echoing all around. "You have no idea who you're challenging."

He flew straight at Killian, who danced and dodged out of the way, playing defense more than offense for the moment.

"Hold on just a little longer, Killian," said Edmund, though he sounded exhausted.

"He can't!" Sven replied with triumph in his voice. Addressing Killian now, he went on, "You've finally managed to shed your humanity, but you still aren't strong enough."

"It's because of my humanity that I'm doing this," Killian answered back. "Because I still have the ability to care about other people."

"Humans are lesser creatures."

"No. I think they're greater. Maybe they don't have wings or telepathy, but at least they're not mindless killing machines constantly seeking out death."

"It is not death that I seek," Sven hissed. And suddenly there were under the vast branches of a great tree—Killian recognized it as the same one he had seen from afar in his dreams. The illusion was powerful, but he knew it was nothing more than a smoke screen; he could still feel Edmund and John in the background.

"What is this place?" Killian asked, mostly just trying to keep Sven talking and distracted.

Sven drew breath to reply but let it out in a scream of rage and pain. The tree vanished in an explosion of light, and then Killian was in total darkness. The change was so sudden that he didn't know where he was. He only knew that John and Edmund and Sven seemed to have gone, and he was alone. Had John died? Was this what happened when he got caught up in that rush of energy as the soul left the body? Killian only realized he was back in his own mind when he heard the air whistling past his ears while he plummeted toward the ground far below. Then he felt something underneath him, supporting him and guiding him to an air current so he could rest and get his bearings back.

"It's okay," came Natalie's voice. But that was all she had time to say before Sven came out of nowhere and barreled into her, almost knocking her out of the air.

"Traitor!" he screamed at Killian, trying to get at him, but Natalie kept inserting herself between them. "Get out of the way, foolish girl! He does not deserve your help. What he deserves is death."

"No. You're the one that deserves that," Killian snarled back.

But it was only talk and Sven knew it; Killian was simply too exhausted to launch another mental assault. So, he focused on guarding himself instead. Natalie helped as best she could, but Sven was much more powerful than either of them. Then Killian heard John, speaking to him and Natalie but blocking out Sven.

"Get yourselves to Crater Ridge now. I'll distract him."

"What about Edmund?" asked Killian.

"He'll kill you!" said Natalie at the exact same time.

"Edmund can handle himself for a little while longer, and so can I. Now go."

As John disappeared from their minds, Sven said, "You have betrayed me! You have betrayed your family!"

"No," Killian replied. "I'm staying loyal to myself, and to what I believe in. I thought you liked that sort of thing. Honor and all that."

He did his best to keep all of Sven's attention on him, giving John the best chance at a surprise attack. Sure enough, before Sven could reply a dark shape wheeled down from above, plowing straight into him.

"Come on," said Natalie as John and Sven shot toward the ground in a tangle of wings and flashing talons. When Killian didn't move, Natalie nudged him none too gently with her beak. "We have to go!"

"We can't just leave him!"

"We have to," she replied, and Killian could feel that her heart was breaking. "I don't like it any more than you do, but we have to."

So they fled, and it was only with great difficulty that Killian stopped himself from looking back, mentally or otherwise.

CHAPTER 18

I t seemed to take them ages to get to Crater Ridge. Killian wanted to stop and rest at the cliff where they slept every night, but Natalie pushed them on.

"It would be too dangerous," she said. "If Sven comes looking for us, that's the first place he'd go."

"He'll know where to find us regardless," Killian reminded her. "We're all basically carrying GPS beacons around inside our heads."

"I'm blocking the signal for both of us."

"I could help."

"I think right now you just need to focus on staying aloft. I don't know what you went through back there, but you're exhausted."

"What happened to Charles and Randall?"

"I didn't see. We didn't know what to think after you three disappeared into John's head, but then you started to fall and Edmund yelled for me to catch you, so I did. I lost track of things after that."

"I hope they're okay. They're not the ones who

betrayed Sven, but he might take his anger out on them anyway."

"What do you mean 'betrayed him'?"

"I mean I fought him off and stopped him from killing John."

"Then it wasn't Sven who turned him back into an odedaud?" Natalie asked.

"No. That was Edmund," Killian replied.

"You're still not telling me everything."

Killian looked inside himself and found that, despite the energy he was exerting just to stay in the air, he was still guarding his innermost thoughts. Mir really had trained him well.

"Who's Mir?"

"Let's just get to Crater Ridge and wait for John and Edmund. They'll be able to explain more than I can."

Natalie asked no more questions, although Killian could still feel her burning curiosity. Killian dug deep, found the power inside himself that he had so recently discovered, and drew from what little remained in his tank. It was just enough to get them to their destination. They both landed, Killian glad of the chance to rest. His eyes slipped closed, but he still swept the surrounding area with his mental lens, looking for any sign of Edmund, John, or Sven. Then he felt Natalie's wall inch higher, and he automatically added his own waning strength to it.

"What is it?" he asked.

"There's somebody else here," she replied. "And not someone from our flock. Whoever it is knows how to guard their mind. I only caught a glimpse, but they're somewhere over there."

Killian focused in on the area she indicated and sensed an unexpected but welcome presence.

"It's okay," he told Natalie. Then, louder, he called, "Mir? Is that you?"

"How did you find me?" asked the other bird, gliding over to them.

"Natalie did," Killian answered.

"Edmund wasn't lying when he said your skills were impressive," Mir said to her.

"Edmund told you about me? I don't understand. Who are you?"

"I am the leader of another flock of odedaud," he replied.

"There are more of us?"

"My flock and Sven's are the only two groups."

"Did Sven know about you?" Natalie asked. "Why didn't he ever tell us?"

"He knew about me, certainly. As to why he never told you, I can't say. Sven and I have a... complicated relationship. He is envious of my territory, while I am content to stay out of his way. I do not want a war with him, but if he makes the first move I will do whatever it takes to defend myself and my family."

"I think he might attack sooner rather than later," Killian said.

"Edmund explained some of the situation, but not everything," said Mir. "He told me someone named John was in danger."

"John used to be part of our flock," Natalie explained. "Earlier tonight he was in a hit-and-run car accident. That's what Sven told us anyway. And then someone stopped to help him and… I don't know what happened after that."

She looked at Killian and he took up the story. "Sven dragged me and Edmund into John's head. We both refused to help him commit murder, so he went to try and do it alone. I got in the way and Edmund changed John back into an odedaud, however that works."

"You fought Sven by yourself?" Natalie asked, sounding awed.

"I couldn't have held him off for much longer."

"What happened after that?" asked Mir.

"We all scattered," Natalie supplied when Killian did not speak. "John told me and Killian to come here, and the last thing we saw was him attacking Sven. I don't know what happened to Edmund or the other two members of our flock."

Silence fell among them, Killian still recovering his strength and Natalie struggling to absorb all she had just been told.

"Are we waiting for someone else to join us?" asked Killian after a while.

"I told Edmund to meet us here, and now I assume John will come as well," Mir answered. "Ah, and here comes the last participant in our little gathering."

Looking around, Killian saw the beam of a flashlight getting steadily closer. The brightness blinded him, so he used his mental eyes to look at the man who was holding it.

"Gavin?" he asked in disbelief.

"Yes. You're looking well, Killian." Then he turned to Mir and added, "Hello, boss."

"I haven't been your boss for a very long time. I

should clarify, Gavin used to be part of my flock," he added for Natalie and Killian's benefit, sensing their confusion.

"Right," said Natalie. "Nice to meet you."

"And you must be Natalie," said Gavin. "The one John couldn't shut up about."

"Really?" She sounded a good deal more cheerful.

Gavin smiled at her briefly, and then turned to Mir again. "Sorry I was late. Had a few loose ends to tie up. Like going to the hospital to see a man who'd been hit by a car." He paused before adding, "Quite a coincidence he got hurt tonight, of all nights."

"What do you mean?" Killian asked.

"I don't know exactly what happened to him but I know he was trying to catch up to Sarah." Gavin looked down into Killian's eyes and said, "She was on her way to the hospital to authorize them to take you off life support."

"She really wanted to give up on me?" Killian asked when he had found his voice again.

"You took a turn for the worse."

"How? John's body stayed the same for almost thirty years."

"John was not a part of Sven's inner circle," Mir broke in. "Separating someone's essence from their body requires an enormous amount of energy, which takes a toll on your human body as well."

"So you mean I'm less human because of what I've been doing?"

"That's a harsh way of looking at it," said Mir, but he didn't deny it.

"When John found out where Sarah was going, he told

Edmund," said Gavin. He glanced at Mir and added, "I assume it was Edmund who reached out to you?"

"Yes," Mir answered. "He told me of his suspicions as you were on your way to meet Sven."

"And Edmund didn't bother to say a word to me?" said Killian, the anger wiping out some of his weariness.

"There wasn't time, and it wouldn't have helped. If anything, it would have put you in more danger," said Mir.

"Why?"

"Because your human emotions would have held you back. Would you really have been able to focus on beating Sven if you were thinking about possibly being stuck in this form forever?"

"I thought you were different," said Killian coldly. "But right now you sound just like him."

Mir did not reply, and Killian sat stewing over things in silence.

"Company incoming," said Natalie eventually, looking west. Two faint shapes were approaching, shapes which soon resolved themselves into the forms of Edmund and John, both looking exhausted but essentially unharmed.

"I'm relieved you made it," said Mir. "Are you all right?"

"We will be," said John.

"Where is Sven?" asked Natalie.

"I don't know," Edmund answered. "But I think we'll be safe from him for a little while. He needs time to recover, just like we do. I'm too weak to search for him right now, let alone fight him again."

"I guess you have done quite a bit tonight," Killian admitted, the weakness in Edmund's voice softening some of his feelings.

"I couldn't have accomplished it without your help. You were incredible. And I am truly sorry for not giving you more time to prepare."

"Right," Killian replied shortly. "Well, at least it's over now."

"On the contrary, it is just beginning," Mir said, and his voice was grave. "This conflict is greater than any of you know."

"So where do we go from here?" Edmund asked.

"If you wish, you can go your own way, avoid choosing a side in the conflict that is to come. But if that is your decision, I should warn you that Sven considers everyone who is not with him to be against him. Or you can come with me to my territory. I can offer you protection, and give you more information about what you would be fighting for."

Mir paused, and then went on, "I do not force this upon any of you. The choice is yours and yours alone. So… which path will you take?"

One by one, they answered.

ACKNOWLEDGMENTS

First word of gratitude goes to everyone who believed in me as I was writing this (my family especially).

Second, thank you to my editor, Josiah Davis. If there are any mistakes remaining in this book, they are mine, not his.

Finally, thank you to BriarsideDesign at SelfPubBook-Covers for my incredible cover.

Made in the USA
Middletown, DE
26 September 2023